Bella Monroe's List of Things That Won't Go Away:

1. The "Dear Jane" letter from my now ex-husband.

2. And that he took the car.

3. And all of our savings.

4. Charlie Fredericks—an ex-cop who's turned Realtor. Somehow he thinks he can sell my house better than I can.... Ha!

5. Debts, debts and more debts. Oh, yes, and a failing business. Fantastic.

6. Charlie Fredericks...again? And now he wants to make a deal to help me renovate the house so I can sell it faster. *Hmm.*

7. Two teenage kids who are both the light of my life and the curse of my loins.

8. Charlie again. Although I'll admit, he *is* a fine-looking man.

9. My ever-growing libido.

10. Hope. *I can't remember the last time I felt this way....*

Dear Reader,

I'm a woman of a certain age and, after many wanderings and intriguing adventures, I decided to sell my house in Vancouver and move back to the little coal-mining town where I was born. I decided to bypass real estate agents in favor of For Sale By Owner—and that wild and wonderful experience became the raw material for *The Family Solution*.

Of course everything about the sale turned out perfectly. Doesn't it always? And I found the ideal house here in Sparwood—but not the one I was first intent on buying. Nothing ended up the way I'd envisioned. It's all so much better, it takes my breath away.

There's a saying: *The way to make God laugh is to tell Him your plans.* I'm a slow learner, because I keep on causing much hilarity in heaven.

I wish you laughter—and love.

Bobby Hutchinson

THE FAMILY SOLUTION
Bobby Hutchinson

For Shirley —
my pal at Curves —
Very best —
Bobby H.

HARLEQUIN®

TORONTO • NEW YORK • LONDON
AMSTERDAM • PARIS • SYDNEY • HAMBURG
STOCKHOLM • ATHENS • TOKYO • MILAN • MADRID
PRAGUE • WARSAW • BUDAPEST • AUCKLAND

ISBN-13: 978-0-373-71439-1
ISBN-10: 0-373-71439-4

THE FAMILY SOLUTION

This is a work of fiction. Names, characters, places and incidents are either the product of the author's imagination or are used fictitiously, and any resemblance to actual persons, living or dead, business establishments, events or locales is entirely coincidental.

This edition published by arrangement with Harlequin Books S.A.

® and TM are trademarks of the publisher. Trademarks indicated with ® are registered in the United States Patent and Trademark Office, the Canadian Trade Marks Office and in other countries.

www.eHarlequin.com

Printed in U.S.A.

ABOUT THE AUTHOR

To alleviate the boredom of training for her first marathon, Bobby Hutchinson made up a story about Pheidippides, the original marathoner, as she ran. She copied it down, submitted it to the short-story contest at Canada's *Chatelaine* magazine, won first prize and became a writer. Today she has over thirty-five published books.

My thanks to Paul Eviston in Vancouver and Bruce Gilmar in Sparwood for real estate information—and for both leading me gently to two signs that said Sold.

PROLOGUE

BELLA JANE MONROE TURNED thirty-seven on October 9.

As consciousness slowly dawned, she had no presentiment that this was the morning her life would change. She simply woke up feeling guilty and remembering too late one of her mother's favorite sayings—which of course Mae Howard had never applied to her own short-lived marriage.

Never go to be bed angry with your husband. Disregarding the source, the advice was solid. Why, Bella wondered, did she only remember good advice after the fact?

Last night she'd been mad enough at Gordon to want to smack him with something heavy. But she wasn't really the violent type, except in her imagination. If she wasn't a fighter, however, then neither was she a lover. She'd come to the conclusion during the past year that she didn't love Gordon any more, which made her feel sad and guilty, and was probably at the root of the problems between them.

Certainly she'd loved him sixteen years ago, when they were married. At least, she was pretty sure she had loved him, even if she wasn't sure exactly when she'd stopped. She was clearer about why, but then she'd made promises that long-ago day—vows that had to do with other things than love.

There was honor, and sickness and health, and worldly goods, not to mention the kids. She was determined that Josh and Kelsey would not grow up the way she had, in a single-parent home. And there was loyalty. Bella prided herself on being loyal.

She opened her eyes, yawned and stretched. Her back was still turned to Gordon's side of the king-size bed, the way it had been when she finally got to sleep. She squinted at the clock and did a double take. Eight forty-seven? *Holy crap.* The alarm hadn't gone off.

The kids would be late for school. Monroe's Hardware wouldn't open on time. Bella groaned and sat up, registering the odd fact that Gordon wasn't snoring beside her. In fact, he wasn't in bed at all, which was a shocker. For the past six months, ever since the business had started going south, he'd refused to get up before ten, which meant she had to drive Kelsey and Josh to school and open the store. It was that and a dozen other irritations that had driven Bella to confront him the night before.

Attack him, actually—*be honest here, Bella.* The discussion had started over something basic.

As long as Gordon wasn't working at the store, Bella thought he could at least figure out something for dinner and make an attempt to have it on the table when the kids got home.

And somehow the whole thing had rapidly escalated into World War III, ending only when he made his standard retreat into stone-cold silence.

She felt a little sick, remembering it. What if Josh and Kelsey had overheard? Teenagers had enough to contend with, without hearing their parents have a meltdown.

A chill October breeze drifted in the open window. The room was freezing, the damp Vancouver air filled with the promise of rain.

Bella dragged herself out of bed, shivering as she slammed the window shut. A piece of yellow lined paper fluttered off Gordon's pillow and landed on the floor. She leaned over and picked it up, one hand pressed against the front of her flannel nightgown in an effort to stay warm. Just for an instant, hope flickered. Gordon had never in living memory admitted he was wrong or said he was sorry. Maybe this time…

"I'm taking off," she read. "You and the kids will be better off without me. I'm sorry about the Volvo and the money in the savings account, but I need them. In return I've signed the house and store over to you—power of attorney is on my desk. Tell the kids I love them. G."

Bella read the note twice, and then a third time, slower, as if it had been written in a foreign language. When the words finally started to make sense, her heart was thudding against her ribs and she heard herself begin to moan.

Her legs buckled, and she sank to her knees on the carpet. Rocking back and forth, she crumpled the note into a ball and threw it across the room.

Betrayal, abandonment, rage—terror. The feelings of desperation poured through her.

She grabbed the neck of her nightgown with both hands and pulled as hard as she could, until the soft fabric tore all the way to the hem, then she ripped it crosswise. She wished it was Gordon's heart she'd just dispatched, but it felt so much more like her own.

CHAPTER ONE

HANDS TREMBLING FROM too much caffeine and not enough sleep, Bella sipped yet another mug of coffee and tried to figure out how to balance a stepladder halfway up the stairs.

It was Sunday morning, ten days, two hours and seventeen minutes since she'd first read The Letter, and when the doorbell rang, relief and anticipation replaced the anxiety that generally sat like a rock in the middle of her chest.

Niki was early, bless her heart. Desperate to unload the newest details of her life into the sympathetic ears of her best friend, Bella hurried to the door and threw it open.

"Morning, Ms. Monroe."

The man on her makeshift front steps was of medium height, of medium weight and with more than medium shoulders, and she'd seen him somewhere before. He had nice eyes, and his broken nose gave his handsome features character. He wore jeans and a denim jacket lined with sheepskin, and the fact that he wasn't dressed in a suit like the other real-estate people she'd encountered in the past week misled Bella, but only until he began to speak.

"I'm Charlie Fredricks. We met the day you came by the real-estate office? You spoke with my brother, Rick." He smiled and extended a large hand, which he obviously intended for her to shake.

Bella tried to swallow her fierce disappointment, and then gave up the attempt to control her temper, which, according to her mother, she'd inherited from her absentee father.

What was it with the men in her life?

"It's Sunday. You do realize that? You people are driving me *nuts*. I have more work than there are hours in the day. Emotionally, I'm a wreck. I've explained to about 227 *other* real-estate idiots from your office why I can't afford your rip-off commissions, and I'm sick to death of being hounded this way."

Somehow forgetting the heavy mug in her hand, she swung an arm to slam the door. Hot coffee flew—some of it hitting her hand. She swore and the stoneware mug went flying, connecting with Charlie Fredricks's forehead with surprising force.

He groaned and staggered backward. The mug fell on the step and shattered. Bella watched in horror as blood trickled down his forehead, even as the coffee stains were spreading across his chest.

"Damn it all to hell," she muttered.

Her hand stung. Would he sue? The thought of a lawsuit on top of everything else made her want to throw herself on the rug and sob. But instead, Bella drew a breath and took hold of his denim jacket.

"Get in here—you're bleeding." She led him inside and closed the door. "I didn't mean to hit you—honestly! I was just closing the door, and I forgot I had coffee in my hand!"

"Closing the door right in my face." He rubbed the sleeve of his jacket across his forehead to staunch the blood that was dripping all over her beige carpet. "I didn't think I'd need hazard insurance on this job."

"Think you could try not to bleed on the rug?" She led the way into the kitchen and pointed at a stool. "Sit down and I'll get something to put on that." She rummaged in a kitchen drawer and came up with a clean dishcloth, which she ran under cold water and then pressed, none too gently, against his forehead.

"Now sit there while I find my first-aid stuff." For that, she had to go upstairs, since there was nothing in the downstairs lavatory except roughed-in plumbing, thanks to her layabout poor excuse of a husband, Gordon.

"Lazy, good-for-nothing…" she muttered, stomping up the stairs.

From behind Josh's bedroom door came the sound of his Xbox.

From behind Kelsey's came the steady, irate hum of complaining, as she no doubt filled in a friend on the subject of her awful mother. And all Bella had done to them today was ask them to help with the painting.

She grabbed antiseptic and Band-Aids and headed back down, but when she got to the kitchen, Charlie What's-his-name wasn't there. She found him in the living room, holding a family photo he'd taken from the fireplace mantel. His jacket was off, and she could see that his blue T-shirt was dotted with spots of crimson.

"Good-looking youngsters. How old are they?"

"Fifteen and thirteen. Give me that." It slipped as she set it facedown on the exposed bricks, shattering the glass, and that felt like the final straw to Bella. "Look, Charlie Fredricks, no one invited you to wander around my house and poke into my things," she said. "You're getting blood all over the house. I'll have to have the carpets cleaned and I can't afford it. Go and sit down, so I can do something about your head, and then you're leaving."

He said quietly, "As a first-aid person, you don't exactly inspire confidence, you know that, Ms.

Monroe?" But then he ambled back to the kitchen and sat on the stool she pointed at.

Bella doused a cotton ball with antiseptic and pressed it firmly against the cut.

He flinched, but didn't say anything.

His hair was a dark chocolate-brown, thick, wavy and a little too long, and it fell onto his forehead and got in the way, so that she had to keep shoving it aside. His eyes were an unusual combination of gray and green, and his eyelashes were kind of nice, she thought, in spite of herself. She pressed a second helping of antiseptic onto the gash.

"Ouch. Owww. Damn it, lady, your bedside manner could stand some work. I didn't ask you to bash me, you know."

"And I don't remember asking you to come to my door and harass me, either." She opened a Band-Aid and tried to cover the gash. "This little cut is too big for a bandage. I need tape and gauze," she muttered. "You sit right there until I get back. No nosing around my house."

"Man, you're tough," he commented as she headed back up the stairs. "And I thought my ex was difficult."

"Yeah, well, maybe she had reasons."

"Mom?" Kelsey stood in the bedroom doorway. "Can I go to the afternoon movie with Brittany? Her dad's going to drive us and pick us up after."

"I thought you were supposed to help me paint."

"Auntie Niki's coming to help you. You don't need me. *Please,* Mom?"

Josh's door opened. "If she gets to go, so do I." At fifteen, his voice was cracking. Most of the time, Bella found it endearing and sad—her baby was growing up. Today, she just felt exasperated.

"I keep telling you two, there's no money for the mall or movies."

"Nana gave us money."

Bella might have known. Her mother doted on her grandchildren.

"How come you didn't tell me?"

"She said it was our little secret," Kelsey said. "She said with Dad away we needed some mad money, to do whatever we wanted. And I want to go to the matinee."

What was the point in trying to make them work? Bella was up against Mae and a united teenage front.

"So go," she said sharply. "Just get out of my sight. And make sure you're back here by suppertime." Even as she snapped at them, she knew it wasn't fair to be so short-tempered, but anger was just about the only thing that kept the tears at bay these days. And she couldn't afford to cry much more.

The kids must have been prepared, because

they were both down the steps and out the door before Bella could make it to the first-aid drawer.

Downstairs, she cut gauze and tape and finally sorted out Charlie's head.

"Your kids were in a real hurry to get out of here," he noted.

She gave him a killer look.

"Not that I blame them," he added. He pointed at the ladder in the hall. "Guess they don't like painting, either, huh?"

"Guess not." She rolled up the gauze and snapped the tape container back together. "That's it, you're mended. Heads always bleed a lot. It's barely a scratch. You'll be fine."

"Yeah, I've noticed that myself. About heads bleeding. I suppose you've patched up a lot of cuts in your time, huh?"

"A fair number." She picked up his jacket and handed it to him. "Sorry about the coffee mug."

"You're not a believer in western hospitality, I take it?"

The doorbell rang and Bella went to answer it.

"Hey, how's it going?" Niki took off her vintage fur and draped it on the coat rack, then gave Bella a hug that almost cracked her ribs. Niki's shoulder-length blond hair had a lavender streak this week and her breasts spilled beguilingly out of the low neckline of her scarlet knit dress. "No word from the scumbag, I take it?"

Bella shook her head, frowned and jerked a thumb in the direction of her battered guest.

Niki raised her eyebrows and walked into the kitchen. "Well, hello there. I thought for a second you were Bella's soon-to-be ex, and I was about to give you a choice piece of my mind."

"No need for that—the lady of the house and I have already gone down that road. I'm Charlie, by the way. How do you do?" He extended a hand, and Niki took it in both of hers, turning it palm up and studying it closely.

"I'm Niki, seeing as how we're only doing first names. Wow, that's some long life line you've got there."

"Oh, yeah? Wish I'd known that when bad guys were shooting at me."

Bella was sure he was looking down the front of Niki's dress. She needed to get him the hell out of here.

"You a drug dealer?" Niki sounded fascinated.

"Nothing so romantic. I was a cop."

"Was?"

Bella was trying to give Niki the signal to lay off her questions, but of course her friend wasn't paying any attention. Niki never did, if there was an attractive man in the vicinity. Bella knew it was all just show, since Niki was devoted to her husband, Tom. But the guys her friend hit on for fun didn't know that.

"I moved on. Now I'm in real estate."

"So you're going to sell Bella's house for her?"

"No, he most emphatically is *not* going to," Bella snapped. "I'm selling it myself. You remember—you were the one who told me to, Niki. You said your uncle Giovanni would have helped me figure out a price, except—"

"Except he's got Alzheimer's," Niki interrupted. "I know, I know. We agreed you'd sell it yourself."

"There you have it." He shrugged. "You ladies for sure know your own minds."

"Have to be on the ball when you're a woman." Niki pointed at the tape and gauze. "What happened to your head?"

"Ms. Monroe and I were having a few words and she chucked a mug at me."

"Go, Bella." Niki gave her a thumbs-up. "Repressed anger leads to illness, and you don't want that."

"It was an accident." Bella scowled at Charlie. "You don't have a concussion, and I patched you up. So you can go now."

Niki went over to him and stroked her finger over his bandaged wound. "Did you know she got a big chunk of your hair trapped inside the tape? Here, let me fix that for you."

"Niki, for cripes sake, lay off, would you? You can't take him home—Tom won't like it."

Niki sighed dramatically. "Sometimes marriage is very limiting." She undid the tape and tenderly freed the hair. "You married, Charlie?"

"Divorced."

"Kids?"

"One daughter. Emma's twenty."

"Which makes you what, forty something? You don't look forty something." Niki gave him a serious look as she patted the bandage back in place. "You don't look a day over thirty. Eight."

"Forty-four." He grinned, obviously pleased with his view down the front of Niki's dress. He had a pirate's grin, Bella thought. That is, if pirates had good dental plans. But then, real-estate salesmen were pirates, weren't they?

He said, "To misquote a famous lady, this is what forty-four looks like."

Niki nodded. "Good old Germaine. What's become of her, anyway?"

"She got herself married," Bella said. "And there went another feminist."

"Oh, marriage is no deterrent to feminism," Niki said. Finished with her Florence Nightingale act, she wandered over to the cupboard and took down two mugs. "What's your daughter's name again, Charlie?"

"Emma. She's in her second year at the University of British Columbia and she wants to be a doctor."

"That's encouraging. We need more women doctors, don't we, Bella? There are some things only a woman understands." Niki filled the mugs with coffee and handed him one.

"He can't stay," Bella said, reaching for the mug a moment too late. He eluded her and took a hefty sip.

"I'm not in any hurry," he said. "Good coffee. Got any cream?"

Niki got a box out of the fridge, adding some cream to her own coffee before she handed it to him. She got two spoons out and gave one to him. They stirred companionably.

She said, "So what kind of career move is that, going from copping to real estate?"

"Not lateral, I'll tell you that." For the first time, Bella could sense he was uneasy. His grin faltered. "So what do you do, Niki?"

"Hair. Nails. On really bad days, bikini waxing." She shuddered. "Yuck. And on the other end of the scale, brows and lashes. Didn't you like being a cop?"

Bella gave up and waited for his answer. Trying to stop Niki was like trying to stop a tank. She'd just roll on until he'd told her everything she wanted to know.

"I liked it fine. It was just time for a career move."

Niki nodded. "Midlife crisis, huh?"

"I guess you could call it that." He downed the rest of his coffee in one long gulp and got to his feet. "I hate to drink and run, but duty calls." He gave Bella a wink. "I know you're dying for me to stay, but I have other unfortunate souls to harass."

"Important work. Don't let us keep you." She was on her feet in an instant.

"Interesting meeting you again, Ms. Monroe. A real pleasure, Niki."

"Likewise." She gave him a seductive smile. "And for God's sake, call her Bella. Ms. Monroe smacks way too much of Marilyn, and we don't need that much drama when we're trying to clean up a house."

Niki paid absolutely no attention to Bella's glares, and fluttered her perfectly manicured hand at Charlie, who saluted and ambled toward the door.

Bella waited until it closed behind him before she got herself a fresh coffee and slumped on her stool.

"God spare me from any more real-estate vultures."

"He said you knew him. Where from?"

"I made the colossal mistake the other day of going into Fredricks Real Estate, over on Dunbar. I thought they might give me some suggestions about selling this place myself, like what price to ask. Instead, they unleashed every salesperson in their office on me, all trying to change my mind and list with them. He's just the latest one. And you weren't exactly helpful. Why were you so friendly?"

Niki clucked her tongue. "Bella, Bella. You're a single lady now and he's a distinct maybe. He's available, doesn't strike me as a serial killer, doesn't reek of liquor, has a job, good teeth and presumably other working body parts, to say nothing of a sense of humor. But you've got to change your attitude, honey. You catch more flies with sugar, my dear old Granny Ruthie used to say."

"You didn't have a dear old granny. Ruthie was a mean old woman who used to dose us with that awful worm medicine and send us out to buy her cigarettes, remember? She never even let us keep the change. We hated her."

"Figure of speech. That weasel in the corner store sold them to us, too. He'd never get away with that these days. What I'm trying to get across to you, sweetie, is that you're not going to find eligible men hanging off lilac bushes, y'know. You have to be a little friendlier. Men like friendlier. And sexy. I don't want to criticize, but that paint all over your arms and neck doesn't do a thing for you—it's in your hair, too. Come over and collect your birthday present, because you need a new do.

And at the moment, you're bordering on anorexic. Aren't you eating?"

Bella put her cup down—one accident a day with coffee was enough. She leaned toward her friend. "Niki. Read my lips. Gordon left me ten days ago, I have debts you wouldn't believe, my kids are acting out, to put it mildly and my mother is threatening to arrive at the door any minute."

"I thought Mae was happy over there in Blue Hair Haven, or whatever it's called."

"She was, until I told her about Gordon. Now she doesn't think I'm capable of raising Josh and Kelsey on my own, and figures we ought to pool resources, seeing that we're both abandoned women. As if I need any more suggestions about decorating and single parenting, or snide remarks about how I drove Gordon away by being a short-tempered shrew."

Niki shook her head. "You? Testy, maybe. What did she give you for your birthday?" Mae's inappropriate gifts had always made them both laugh.

"She outdid herself." Bella opened the catch-all drawer and pulled out a thick book. "Ta-da."

Niki took it. *The Dummy's Guide to Living Well?* She snorted, and then erupted into giggles. "She has outdone herself this time."

Bella had to smile. "I thought so. *The Dummy's Guide to Poverty* might have been a wiser choice." She grew sober, remembering how close she was to bankruptcy. "I had no idea how much in debt we are. Gordon was an accountant, and he was supposed to be managing the money. Instead, he'd let the house mortgage lapse, the lease on the store is three months in arrears and our overdraft is maxed out. The business is in the toilet, and there's nothing to do but shut it down. I have to somehow sell off what stock I can and get this place in good enough shape to sell. And I have to do it all fast, because *I have no money.*"

"You didn't tell Charlie boy that, I hope? Because guys tend to get a wee bit nervous if you mention money right off the bat."

"Of course I didn't." Actually, Bella wasn't too sure *what* she'd said to him. She was pretty much nuts these days, and not responsible for what came out of her mouth. "Anyhow, there is no way I want anything to do with another man unless he's a filthy rich plumber slash handyman slash landscape gardener, who loves to paint and has his own home." She ran out of breath and gulped. "So no more men. Not now, and probably not ever."

Niki wasn't impressed. "You'll change your mind. Your libido will kick in, and when it does you'll remember this hunky real-estate cop and regret the way you acted."

"Not in this lifetime. Now, are you going to help me paint and let me whine some more about my problems, or are you just going to keep lecturing me about hormones?"

"Whine away. And do you have something truly awful—like what you're wearing—that I can change into? Because I don't want to get paint on this dress. It's pretty hot, and it's going to drive Tom crazy. I just bought it at the New to You on Dunbar. This end of town is a gold mine for expensive secondhand clothes."

"I'll get you that purple track suit of mine."

Niki groaned. "If I should fall off the ladder wearing it, do not let the paramedics in the door until you get me back into my dress."

"You are so vain."

"I know. It's one of my strengths."

Bella surprised herself and laughed.

Niki looked pleased. "There now, that wasn't so hard, was it?"

"Not around you, you whacko." Bella put an arm around Niki's shoulders and hugged her tight. "I'm so glad you're here. The thought of painting the downstairs in eight hours or less makes me dizzy and sick."

"It's not the painting that's doing that, it's hunger. When did you last eat a whole mess of greasy, fried junk food?"

"That would have been the day before Gordon left, when we ordered pizza and chicken wings. Can't afford order-in anymore."

"Yeah, well, I'm ordering in right now. You want anchovies? Pineapple? Zucchini? My treat, Mrs. Angelino tipped me forty bucks for making her hair look thick. And I refuse to paint on an empty stomach."

"No anchovies. Pineapple's fine. How'd you manage that? The thick hair thing, I mean."

"There's this polymer stuff, that coats each strand and puffs it up, at least until you wash it again, but Mrs. Angelino's from the old school. She only washes her hair once every two weeks or so, when it starts to smell, so she's good to go for a while."

Niki dialed and ordered two extra-large, loaded. She donned Bella's purple track suit and set to work on the dining-room wall, first painting a four-letter word across it, so she'd have to finish it before the kids got back.

When the pizza arrived, Bella found she was actually hungry.

Chomping down on her second slice, she told Niki about the harmonica.

"I bought it for myself, for my birthday. The day before, actually. I was reading the astrology column and found out I was born on the same day as John Lennon and Jackson Browne. I probably should have returned it—it was expensive—but I've been blowing in it every night, so it's too late now. I can play 'Three Blind Mice.' Want to hear?"

Niki shuddered. "Not if I can avoid it. What made you go for a mouth organ? My uncle Popeye used to play one, remember?"

Bella nodded. "So did my dad. He played and I'd dance."

"You were so close to him. Weird you never heard from him after he left."

"Out of sight, out of mind, I guess." When Bella was fifteen, Oscar Howard had left Mae and waltzed off into the Florida sunshine with Dinah Flynn, the neighborhood widow slash home wrecker, never to be heard from again.

Long time ago, Bella, she reminded herself now. *Don't go there. Sufficient unto the moment is the pain thereof.*

She and Niki ate and talked and painted for the rest of the afternoon, and when first Kelsey and then Josh arrived home, the teens were so happy to see Niki and the leftover pizza they even forgot to be rude.

If only she could bottle essence of Niki, Bella thought later that evening. She knew her friend had challenges of her own—Niki and Tom wanted a big family, but after twelve years of marriage and many consultations with experts, they still hadn't managed to get pregnant. Niki was now thirty-nine, and time was running out. She joked about each procedure she went through, making it sound ludicrous and funny, and she never complained.

The problems she'd started out with that morning were still the same, Bella thought, sinking into a tub of scented hot water. They just seemed a lot less important after a healthy dose of her friend's slightly outrageous humor.

Bella even chuckled, remembering the fiasco with the coffee cup and the real-estate cop. Charlie boy, Niki had called him.

At least she didn't have to worry about Charlie boy ever coming back.

CHAPTER TWO

HE WAS GOING TO HAVE TO find a way to soften her up, Charlie decided as he'd climbed into his battered Ford truck and backed out of Bella's driveway. He was going to get the listing for her house, even if it damn near killed him.

"It's an FSBO, a tough one," Rick had warned, using the acronym that meant for sale by owner. "The location's prime, and there's a thousand dollar bonus in it for anybody who changes her mind. Why not give it a shot, bro?"

Charlie knew that everyone else in the office had already tried to get the listing. Being low man on the totem pole, he also knew they were likely laying bets with Rick that he, the new boy, couldn't change the lady's mind, either.

Charlie longed to prove them wrong. It wasn't that he had a knack for selling real estate. So far, he pretty much hated it. He was a lousy salesman and he knew it. He was far too inclined to point out water stains on the ceiling and signs of dry rot in the attic. But he had to earn a living, and the career options for an ex-cop who was also a recovering alcoholic, had alimony payments to meet and a daughter in university, weren't good.

He needed a sale, and he needed it soon. Vancouver real estate was hot; everybody knew that. As Rick had told him far too many times, here was his chance to get out of the financial hole he'd dug for himself since he left the police force. His brother had never said it, but Charlie was all too aware that he also needed to pay back the sizable amount he'd borrowed from Rick. Becoming a licensed real-estate agent didn't come cheap, and Rick had been generous.

So Charlie had screwed up his courage and knocked on the lady's door.

He fingered the gash on his forehead and grinned. Spunky, he'd give her that. And sexy— there was something about the way she moved. Skinny. Stubborn. Intense. Challenging. He needed to figure out some angle that would break through her defenses.

That house of hers needed work. She was okay with a paintbrush, but he hadn't noticed any carpentry tools around. She wouldn't be painting it herself if she could afford to hire someone. And her husband had done a runner. Surely there were all sorts of possibilities. He just had to use his imagination, which was about all he had for collateral.

THE FOLLOWING THURSDAY afternoon, Bella was in the washroom at Monroe's, splashing cold water on her face in an attempt to wake herself up enough to get through to closing time in an hour and a half. She'd started falling asleep in the afternoon, head down on the counter, dozing on the receipt forms. She still wasn't sleeping at night, but at least she could now play three songs on the harmonica she'd bought for her birthday. "Golden Slippers" had been especially tough, but she'd conquered it.

Her body was telling her that naps were in order, but taking them at the store wasn't exactly reassuring to the slow but steady stream of customers the closeout sale had attracted.

From the bathroom she heard the ding that told her another customer had just come in. She hastily dried her face and curled her eyelashes. At least that might make her look semiconscious.

She emerged to find Charlie Fredricks standing in front of the pyramid of paint cans she'd erected in the middle of the room.

Bella walked toward him and stopped just inside what should be his comfort zone. She knew from experience that was one sure way of making troublesome customers head for the door.

"Can I help you?" She made herself meet his gray-green eyes—arresting eyes for a guy with such dark hair, she thought again.

"I think we can help each other."

"Oh, yeah? And just what makes you think that?"

"You're closing out, right?" He pointed at the bright red sign in the window.

"Whatever gave you that idea?" Her sarcasm was thick as jam.

He gave her a steady look. "Do you want to discuss business or just trade insults?"

"What sort of business? Because if this has anything to do with you selling my house, I'm not interested."

One of his eyebrows went up. "You're not interested in selling your house?"

She put her hands on nonexistent hips. "Don't play word games, I'm not in the mood."

"Okay, here's the deal. I'm the low man at my brother's agency, and I've been given the listings that nobody can move. Shotgun shacks, Rick calls them, because it would mean holding a buyer at gunpoint to get an offer. There are three of them, and they all need work, to put it mildly."

"Who owns them? Why isn't the owner fixing them up?"

"They're all owned by an absentee landlord. He lives elsewhere, and he's been renting these dumps out. Now that real estate is high, he wants to unload them, and I'd like to sell them, if only to spite the ones at the office who think I'm riding on my brother's coattails." He moved away from her, seemingly intent on a rack of screwdrivers.

"Are you?" She boosted herself up on the counter. This was getting interesting.

He shrugged. He had good shoulders under that denim jacket, and she was relieved to see he'd gotten the bloodstains out. "At the moment, yeah, after a fashion. My brother paid for my real-estate course. See, if I move these babies, the owner will give us listings on other properties he owns, more expensive properties. Problem is, he wants top dollar for them."

"And Rick will benefit if you make this guy happy."

"I'll benefit, too. I'll earn the commissions. I've shown them lots of times to people who think they want a fixer-upper, but these go way beyond the basics."

"So they're more like tear-downers?"

He blew out a frustrated breath. "A couple of developers have looked at them with the thought of tearing them down, but the owner wants too much for them to make it feasible. So the only answer is make them look better."

He turned and came back to where she sat, putting one hand on either side of her. Clearly, perching on the counter had been a tactical mistake. Maybe she was higher than Charlie, but he was way too close. She could see how thick his hair grew on top of his head. And he smelled very pleasantly of coffee and soap.

"I don't have a clue about colors and decorating," he admitted, looking straight into her eyes. "And I can't stand painting. But I *can* do minor repairs, carpentry, some electrical work and plumbing." He took his hands away and drew in a deep breath. "So this is what I thought. You need to sell your house, but it could use a bit of work, too. It looked to me as if you're pretty good with a paintbrush—I liked what you were doing to your walls that day." A grin came and went. "What I saw of them before you booted me out on my ass, that is. But that so-called powder room of yours should really be finished, your landscaping is non-existent and the kitchen could stand backsplash tile and some molding."

Gordon had wanted the house. The contractor who built it had gone bankrupt and the asking price had been well below market value, because it wasn't finished. She wasn't about to tell Charlie all that. Instead she tried for righteous indignation. "You nosed around quite a bit while I was up-stairs."

"What can I say?" He'd probably used that crooked grin before to get his way. "I'm a curious guy, and I'm also pretty good with landscaping. So here's the deal, Bella. I can call you Bella, right?"

"Suit yourself."

"If you supply the paint for my listings and do some of the scut work to help me spruce them up a bit, I'll do what I can with your garden and also put in a toilet and shower for you. I can show you how to tile. It's a valuable thing to learn."

Bella didn't answer right away. She got down from the counter and stood looking at him, wondering what his ulterior motive was. He had to have one. People didn't just wander in off the street with offers to help her solve some of her immediate problems.

"How come you don't just hire painters for those shotgun houses? There's lots of painters around. I have a list as long as your arm." She just couldn't afford to hire them herself.

"Same reason you don't. I don't have a whole helluva lot of spare change at the moment."

"How come? You were a cop—don't you have a pension? And everyone says the real-estate market's hot in Vancouver now. I thought all Realtors were practically millionaires."

"Think again. Selling real estate is no easy road. Sure, I wrote my exam and passed the course, but you need contacts. You need listings. You need clients. You also need a 'patter,' which I seem to lack, according to my wildly successful brother."

"Too honest?" She meant it to be sarcastic.

He squinted at her and nodded. "Could be."

"So what about that solid pension?"

"I didn't have pensionable service. I worked for a contractor after I left the force, doing rough laboring jobs to meet expenses. See, I have a daughter in university and an ex who isn't working. All of which means I don't have much of a bankroll."

Okay. God knows Bella could understand being broke. She wondered what his reasons were for leaving the police force to work as a laborer, but she didn't ask. Even in her present state of mind, that felt too much like prying.

She thought over what he was suggesting. "I don't have a lot of spare time," she finally said. "The store will close at the end of the month, which is about twelve days from now, and then I'll be unemployed. But until then…" She gestured with an arm. "I don't have employees. I have to be here."

"Time is one thing I do have," he said with a smile, flashing those good straight teeth. "So I could start working at your house during the day, while you're here. Unless you figure I'd walk off with the silverware."

"Huh. If I'd had any, Gordon would have taken it," she snapped.

"Gordon being your husband?"

"My so-called husband. Soon to be ex, if I can locate him to serve him papers. And get the damn Volvo back."

"He took your car?"

The familiar sense of outrage returned. "The brand-new car we leased together. He drove off with it, along with every last cent we had, plus a bundle he got from our charge cards."

"So you're stuck with the lease payments."

"Right. And the mortgage, and the rent, and the overdue invoices, and the credit-card debt. And he *knew* the business was doomed." She could hear a hint of hysteria creeping into her voice. "There's my kids' dental bills, groceries, school fees…"

He whistled. "Gordon sounds like someone you're well rid of."

"Thank you. You're a very perceptive man." Bella realized she was smiling at him, and quickly scowled instead. What did she know about him, really?

"I still have contacts, and I could probably help you find him if you wanted to."

Now that was interesting. "You could? I really want to get that Volvo back. As far as Gordon goes, he can stay lost for all I care. But I think it's a case of find him, find the car."

"Where do you figure he is?"

"Mexico. He lived down there before we were married, and he's fluent in Spanish." It was one thing they'd had in common, their interest in the language. In fact, it was how they'd met, at a night-school class. He'd taught her how to swear in Spanish.

"Write down all the particulars."

She grabbed a pad and pen and scribbled down age, weight, height and name.

"Big country. Any location come to mind?"

"West coast, I'd guess. He spent time in the Puerto Vallarta area before we were married. And we went there for our honeymoon."

Bella handed him the paper, with Gordon's full name and description, and the Volvo's license plate number and color.

"I'll need a photo."

"Damn, I tore them all up and burned them."

He raised his eyebrows.

"Kidding. Okay, I can hunt one up."

"A minute ago you were looking at me as if I was pulling a con." Charlie laughed at her surprised expression. "You know, your face really is an open book."

He pulled out his wallet. "Here's my driver's license, my Realtor's ID, my social insurance number. I'll give you my brother's cell number, my mother's name *and* my home address. You're welcome to check me out. In fact, being a former cop, I'd recommend you do exactly that."

Bella glanced at the pile of cards, but only for a moment.

"I don't need these. All I have to do is call my

mother and give her your name and she'll know everything about you in ten minutes, including whether or not you dye your hair. She has an amazing network of blue-haired sleuths."

He stuck his wallet back in his pocket. "Whatever works for you. I just want you to know I'm a man of my word."

"Yeah? Well, it doesn't run in the family, then." Bella's voice hardened. "I told your brother up front I was selling my own house, and he said no problem—he'd help me with pricing. Public service, he said. And then he sent every real-estate person in Greater Vancouver after me."

Charlie nodded. "Rick tends to be a bit overenthusiastic about his work."

"No kidding." A customer had come in, but for the moment he was browsing among the nails and screws. "How did you end up working for him? I mean, wouldn't it be less stressful with strangers?"

Charlie glanced at the customer and lowered his voice. "Probably. Unfortunately, no other person recognized my incredible potential."

"You couldn't get a job anywhere else."

His smile was rueful. "You could say that. So, Bella Monroe, what's your decision on my really excellent proposal?"

She looked at him seriously. She knew you couldn't tell by a person's appearance whether he was honest or not, but you could tell whether or not he might recognize the business end of a shovel and a hammer.

She liked the way Charlie met her eyes and held her gaze. His face was weathered, good-humored and lived-in, with smile lines radiating out from his mouth and bracketing his eyes. She liked the fact that he looked strong and that his nails weren't manicured—in fact, several of them were cracked and all of them were cut short. His big hands looked as if he'd done his share of manual labor. And he didn't have any sign of a potbelly, the soft, little kind that Gordon had been working on.

Quite emphatically not. This guy's body tapered in quite an interesting fashion down from his significant chest, inside its checked green shirt, into narrow blue jeans worn low on his hips. Not designer jeans; these looked more like the kind you bought at the Army and Navy. Utilitarian.

She said slowly, "I guess we could give it a try. When would you start?"

He shrugged. "No time like the present. I could go over to your place right now, take some measurements in that bathroom and figure out what we're going to need in the way of materials." He glanced around. "You've probably got most of the stuff we'll need right here. I can pick up the rest at Foster's."

She gave him a look. "Wash your mouth. I'd drive to Richmond for an hour in rush-hour traffic to buy a single washer rather than shop at Foster's. They're the reason I'm being forced out of business. A small hardware store like this can't compete with a big-box store like that."

He shrugged. "A guy I know says we never know what anything is for. Maybe what seems a disaster for you right now might turn out okay in the long run."

"Oh, yeah? My mother has some of those sayings, too, such as, what doesn't kill you makes you stronger. Which makes me want to be sick."

His laugh was low and deep and even gentle, and sounded as if he meant it. As if he was genuinely amused. But amused or not, there was no way she was handing over house keys to a relative stranger. She told him so.

"I can understand that—it's wise on your part. How about I go over there and assess the landscaping issue, then? I didn't take a close look the other day, but I did get the general impression it was sort of like an undeveloped parking lot."

"The guy who was building it went bankrupt before he could finish. My soon-to-be ex wanted to live in a posh neighborhood, and that about sums it up." What harm could it do to have him look around outside? "I'll be home in—" She squinted at the clock. "Less than an hour. My kids should be there around the same time. We can make a list of supplies, then. Do you happen to have a pick-up?" Monroe's had people with trucks who would deliver orders, but using them was expensive.

"I do, lived-in but reliable. See you in an hour."

The minute he was gone, she had second thoughts. If Charlie did what he said and she managed to sell the house, she'd be too busy finding a place to rent and getting settled to do much painting for him. And how many houses was he talking about here? Just the three he'd mentioned, or had she just made a commitment that could last the rest of her natural life?

The good thing was she hadn't signed anything.

The bad thing; neither had he.

CHAPTER THREE

WHEN SHE DROVE up to her house an hour later, a battered old blue Ford pickup was parked at the curb and a red wheelbarrow was positioned beside Charlie Fredricks, who was already digging, turning over clods of earth and putting them into the barrow.

"Hey," he called cheerfully. He'd stripped off his green shirt and put on a ratty old, long-sleeved tee. His pants were different, too—jeans still, but old and holey in the knees. He'd changed into brown, well-worn work boots.

"What are you doing?" She eyed the growing pile of clods.

"Making a berm, first one over there and then we'll see." His voice was excited, eager. "You have to imagine a garden as a series of rooms. I thought we'd make this the entrance hall, raised beds of flowers, trees along here to shelter the sidewalk… Which is going to be shaped irregularly, winding slowly to the front door. It makes it interesting for guests. And it's good feng shui."

Entrance hall? Feng shui? She glanced at him, thinking he must be joking, but he looked as serious as he ever did—which wasn't very. His face was so good-humored that he always seemed on the verge of a smile. Bella told herself she found that irritating. Nobody could be in a good mood all the time.

"Your youngsters are in the house. I suggested they might want to help, but they weren't too enthusiastic."

No kidding. Getting them to do anything remotely productive these days was almost more effort than it was worth.

"I'll see if I can change their minds about that." Bella decided she'd rout them out and do some digging herself before dinner. It would be good to do something out of doors, together. The day was typically overcast, but it wasn't cold and it wasn't raining, both of which were bonuses.

Inside the front door, she tripped over Kelsey's book bag and then kicked aside Josh's trainers. A trail of cookie crumbs and tortilla chips led from the kitchen to the den. Bella followed.

Josh was sprawled on the sofa, television turned up to an earsplitting level as a NASCAR race unfolded. Two empty soda cans, a flattened milk carton and discarded cookie package lay on the carpet, along with more crumbs.

Bella picked up the remote and turned off the TV.

"Hey." Josh sat up. "Chill, Mom. I was watching that."

"You can watch television later. Right now I'd like you to pick up this mess, put on some old clothes and come outside. We're all going to work in the garden."

"Says who?" His tone was verging on insolent. "The dude out there with the old truck?"

"Says me." Determined not to lose her patience, Bella tried reason. "I have to sell this house, and in order to do that and make some money so we can move and keep on buying groceries, it has to be landscaped. I don't know how to do anything with a garden, but Mr. Fredricks has offered to help. C'mon, it could even be fun."

"I've got homework."

"Well, you weren't exactly working on it. You can do your homework after dinner."

Muttering under his breath, Josh headed for the stairs. Bella looked at the mess he was leaving behind and decided one battle at a time was just about enough.

Upstairs, Kelsey's door was closed. When there was no answer in response to her knock, Bella opened it. Piles of clothing covered the floor. Kelsey reclined against her pillows on the unmade bed, grubby shoes resting on the sheets. She was eating chocolate ice cream and was listening to her iPod. Until Bella was standing over her, she didn't even notice her mother was there.

Kelsey slowly removed the ear buds.

"Yes, Mother?" She took another spoonful of ice cream and raised one eyebrow.

A scant year ago, when she was twelve, Kelsey had still hugged Bella at bedtime and even kissed her goodbye before leaving for school. At thirteen, she'd become something of a changeling, who made no secret of the fact that she had no desire to be in the same room with her mother. The best Bella could expect these days was strained politeness.

"This room is a pigsty." She hadn't intended to say that, but the handmade, black velvet quilt Kelsey had begged for last Christmas was tossed into a corner, and the closet door was open, revealing a nest of tumbled clothing, shoes and damp bath towels. And was that Bella's pink cashmere sweater rolled in a ball on the dresser? She walked over to reclaim it, and saw it had a huge stain across the front, something that looked like ink.

"This is my best sweater. What did you do to this, Kelsey, use it as a blotter?"

Her daughter shrugged. "So, did you come in here just to rail at me?"

"No, I did not." Bella tried for a calming breath. "Get up and put some old clothes on. We're going to dig up the front yard and plant a garden."

"Garden? No, thanks." Kelsey screwed her face into an expression of disgust. "Besides, nobody does their own *gardening,* Mother."

"You're wrong there. Lots of our neighbors on Maple Street used to grow gardens." Bella felt homesick for their old neighborhood. She felt homesick for their old *life.* "I'll bet lots of people here do, too. You just can't see them behind those huge hedges. Prince Charles is a gardener, for heaven's sake."

"Yeah, right. I'll bet Prince William doesn't have a thing for shovels and stuff."

"Well, unfortunately for you, you're not Prince William. So put that ice cream carton in the garbage before it does any more damage, and from now on, do *not* lie on that bed with your shoes on. I'll expect you outside in ten minutes."

Bella got out before she lost it. Barely.

But her own bedroom wasn't that much of an improvement over Kelsey's, she noted. Empty coffee cups littered the floor beside the bed and a bottle of melatonin lay on its side on the bedside table.

She took off her work clothes—cords and a sweater—and put on older cords and a tee, topping it off with the purple, long-sleeved sweatshirt Niki had complained about last Sunday. It had paint splotches, but what the heck? It was fine for digging dirt.

Kelsey and Josh were waiting in the front hall. They might have looked slightly more cheerful if they were going to prison. Bella felt sorry for them.

Their lives had changed almost as much as hers had. But they were all just going to have to get used to it.

She led the way out the door and down the steps. Charlie was still effortlessly moving piles of dirt from one area to another. He waved cheerfully, and Bella introduced her kids.

"Josh, Kelsey, this is Mr. Fredricks."

"Call me Charlie. Pleased to meet you," he said.

Josh and Kelsey didn't reply.

Bella was about to call them on their lack of manners when Charlie said, "There's shovels in the truck. You can start digging out the base for the sidewalk, marked out with that yellow cord. It needs to be six inches deep and relatively even. When we get it dug, I'll put in forms for the concrete."

Sure enough, two parallel yellow cords stretched in a gently curving line from the edge of the property to the front door.

Josh muttered, "A sidewalk? Is this guy nuts?"

Kelsey huffed, "Daddy would never make me do this."

Too true. Daddy never did anything himself.

Bella led the way to the truck and lifted three long-handled spades from the bed. She distributed them and tried to inject enthusiasm into her tone. "Come on, let's get started. How hard can it be?"

Within minutes, she found out. Charlie came over and showed them how to sink the spade into the ground by holding the handle tight and jumping on the blade. He made it look simple.

"Make your cuts on a slight angle, and try to make the clumps of sod a uniform shape," he instructed, handing the shovel back to Bella. "You try it. You might want to find some work gloves first, though."

"I don't think I have any."

He walked over to the truck, rummaged under the front seat and then handed her a filthy pair of gloves. Grimacing, she slipped them on.

The first time she tried to cut the sod, she slipped off the side of the shovel and gouged her ankle. It hurt, but, determined to set a good example, she ignored the pain and tried again. This time, the shovel penetrated the earth three inches, and she felt the reverberation all the way up to her skull.

"Why don't you give it a go, son?" Charlie gestured at Josh, who slowly let go of his shovel. It fell to the ground, narrowly missing Charlie's foot.

"Last time I checked, you weren't my father," Josh said.

Charlie stared at him briefly, then nodded. "You're right, that was patronizing. I apologize."

After a tense moment, Bella said sharply, "Josh. I didn't raise you to be rude."

With obvious reluctance, he shook Charlie's outstretched hand, and then everyone breathed again.

"Okay, let's start over," Charlie said. "How about taking a stab at digging out this sidewalk, Josh?" He reached down, picked up the shovel and held it out.

Josh accepted the shovel, positioned it and stepped down hard. A clump of earth came free, and he lobbed it into the wheelbarrow with energy probably generated by rage.

Charlie ignored Josh's temper. He turned back to what he'd been doing, and Bella went back to trying to get her shovel to sink more than an inch into the ground. Kelsey made her own halfhearted effort, and when it didn't work, she started back toward the house.

"Kelsey, you can come over here and start piling these blocks up in a berm if you want," Charlie called to her.

"I don't want to, and I have no idea what he's talking about," she said in an undertone.

"Go, and be polite," Bella ordered. "He'll explain."

With the speed of a caterpillar, the girl made her way across the yard. Charlie began talking to her, and soon Kelsey was gingerly lifting clods of earth and building them into a long, irregularly shaped hillock.

For the next hour, Bella did her best to establish a work ethic for her children. Her arms ached, her foot still hurt from the shovel and her back was sore from heaving clods of earth into the wheelbarrow, but she persevered until exhaustion got the best of her.

"I think that's enough for today," she finally gasped, glancing at her watch and trying to pretend she wasn't on the verge of a heart attack. "I'll just... I'll go in and make some dinner." Hoping he'd refuse, she added without enthusiasm, "Will you join us, Charlie?" After the work he'd accomplished in spite of their help, she really had no choice except to invite him.

"Thanks, that would be great."

"Mom, can I come in with you?" Kelsey, as dirty as Bella had ever seen her, gave her a beseeching glance. "*Please*, Mom?"

"Sure." Bella glanced over at Josh. He still looked grim, but he was methodically driving the shovel into the ground and digging out clumps. Sweat was running down his forehead.

"Okay, dinner in about an hour, men." She was trying to figure out just what dinner might consist of, and she was failing miserably.

"C'mon, Kelsey." As they made their way into the house, Bella thought it was probably the first time in months her daughter had looked eager to go anywhere with her.

Bella muttered under her breath, "Now what am I going to make?" The cupboards were close to bare and she had no money to order pizza.

"There's hamburger in the freezer," Kelsey said. "We could make that stuff with macaroni and tomatoes and cheese that you used to cook sometimes when we were little."

Bella thought she'd pass out from shock. Kelsey, noticing frozen hamburger? Suggesting a dinner menu?

"I just happened to see the package when I was getting ice cream," she said in a defensive tone.

"I'm glad you did," Bella told her. "Shipwreck, that stuff was called." Perfect for their current situation. And it was one of the very few things she actually knew how to make without a cookbook. "That's a great idea. Let's wash up and get started."

"I can't, Mom." The whine was back. "I have homework. And I'm writing Daddy a letter, for when we know his new address."

"Right. Well, you can finish all that the minute we're done eating, and I'll get Josh to help me with dishes. You did volunteer to help make dinner, Kelsey, and I'm holding you to it. You can chop onions and start browning them, while I thaw the meat and cook macaroni."

Kelsey pulled a face and held out her soil-stained hands. "After I have a shower, right?"

"That's not a bad idea. I'm filthy myself."

By the time Charlie and Josh came in to wash up, Bella had pulled together a meal with Kelsey's help. They'd set out the food on the island in the kitchen, and had actually had a peaceful, productive conversation about how best to chop onions and brown hamburger.

"This is great," Charlie enthused, reaching for another of the baking powder biscuits Kelsey had whipped up at the last minute. Bella had watched her in amazement, wondering where this self-confident young cook had sprung from.

"We learned to make them in school," Kelsey explained. "They're, like, soooo easy."

"I pretty much live on takeout or frozen dinners, so having a home-cooked meal is a real treat," Charlie remarked, slathering butter on a biscuit.

"I don't really do much cooking myself," Bella had to confess.

"No kidding, Mom," Josh agreed. "You haven't made this stuff in a long time."

"Glad you like it." She hadn't made anything from scratch in ages. Bella, too, had been relying heavily on takeout and frozen dinners.

Being Mae's daughter, she'd never really learned to cook, apart from a limited number of dishes along the lines of shipwreck. Her mom had alternately nagged Bella about being too skinny and then produced dishes that were all but inedible.

And lately, Bella had felt too stressed and over-worked and angry with Gordon to concoct even one of her simplest standbys. Which was ironic, because now, when she was *really* stressed and overworked, making a meal from inexpensive ingredients was a financial necessity.

"Josh," Charlie said when they were done eating, "where's that list we made of materials? I forgot to add bonemeal and we'll need that to give the new trees and bushes a head start when we put them in the ground."

Josh pulled a small notebook out of his pocket and scribbled in it, then handed it to Charlie.

"I have a meeting tomorrow morning, but maybe you want to come with me after school to pick this stuff up?"

Josh shook his head. "Can't. Basketball practice," he said.

"What position do you play?"

"Center."

"Your team win any games?"

"About half. We've got a good coach, but a lot of the guys don't play very hard." Josh suddenly remembered to be bored. "I'm only doing it because we get extra credits for sports. It's basically a dumb game."

"It can be rough, that's for sure. That's how I got my nose broken the first time. What sports do you really enjoy?"

"Squash. But we don't have any squash courts at school."

Bella knew Josh hadn't played squash more than a half-dozen times. He was only mentioning it because Gordon had repeatedly said how good he'd been at the game. Not that Gordon had played more than a dozen times, either, as far as Bella could remember. And never with Josh.

Charlie said, "Rick belongs to the Point Grey Athletic Club, and they have courts there. Maybe you'd like to have a game sometime?"

The teen shrugged, concentrating on his empty plate. "Yeah. I guess. Maybe. Sometime. Can I be excused, Mom?"

"Yes, and please load the dishes in the dishwasher for me. And could you wash the pots by hand? Kelsey helped make the meal, and I told her you'd do cleanup."

"Ahh, mom. I've got homework."

Bella raised her eyebrows. "Strange, how whenever I have a job for you to do, you remember your homework."

"Yeah, well, you're always on me to get good grades, right?"

Charlie stood up and began stacking dishes. "How about I give you a hand? That way it won't take long."

"I can do it," Josh muttered.

"No problem. Where are the garbage bags?"

It was obvious Josh didn't want Charlie helping, but there wasn't much he could do about it. Sullenly, he banged pots into the sink as Charlie scraped and rinsed plates for the dishwasher. Kelsey beat a fast retreat up the stairs.

Way too tired to get involved in any more domestic skirmishes, Bella poured herself a cup of coffee and slunk into the living room.

"I'll come and join you as soon as we're done," Charlie promised.

That wasn't exactly what she'd had in mind. She'd been hoping he'd leave right after dinner, but just like with Josh, there wasn't a lot she could do about it. She sank into an armchair and propped her feet on a stool.

She was beginning to ache in places she'd never noticed before, when Charlie came in and made himself comfortable on the sofa. He'd changed his work clothes for his clean jeans and shirt before dinner, and he'd used a wet comb on his hair; the track marks still showed.

Now, if she were Niki, she'd label him hot. Lucky she wasn't the least bit interested.

"I drew up a master plan for your garden," he said, pulling a folded sheet of paper from his pocket. "Come over and have a look, and see what you think." He patted the sofa.

Bella got up and sat beside him, a reasonable distance away.

"I thought we'd make it as low-maintenance as possible, since that's always a good selling point. These days, people don't have time to devote to a garden that requires a lot of upkeep. So we'll use trees and bushes that are indigenous to the coast, we'll put down bark mulch and install underground sprinklers. No lawn, no mowing, and not even many weeds. What do you think?"

Bella peered at the paper in his hands. She could smell him—a mélange of soap, some residual sweat and essence of Charlie.

Pheromones. Niki had told her all about them. The little buggers were working overtime right now.

Bella said, "A sprinkler system sounds expensive."

"I know a guy who'll put it in for a reasonable price."

"Even reasonable is going to be way beyond my budget."

"Well, maybe we can work some sort of a trade with him."

"As in...?" She was so worn out, she found herself thinking of making a joke about sexual favors. As if anyone would consider her current body highly desirable. Always on the skinny side, she'd lost seven or eight pounds over the last few weeks. And what was left of her chest struck her as rather sad.

Yet, the thought of what a man would be doing messing with her chest or pelvic bones still sent warmth rushing to her nether regions. And not just any man. It was ridiculous to be so aware of Charlie. They were simply sitting on a sofa, his right leg a good foot away from her left leg. It went to prove that basic sexual instincts were hot-wired in.

Fortunately, Charlie was oblivious to her X-rated thinking. "I'd have to talk to him, figure out what he needs that we might be able to supply," he mused. "You've probably got plastic pipe and other stuff at the hardware store he could use."

"I do have plastic pipe for irrigation, and some of the valves, as well."

"Great. But we'll need to buy plants and flowers and trees, although I'll get what I can for free. I know a gardener who often has stuff he's discarding. Plus, we'll need ready mix for the sidewalk."

"How much will that come to?"

"Maybe three, four thousand, for both cement and plantings. But the difference it will make in the selling price of your house will be in the tens of thousands."

Bella gulped. There were always going to be expenses she couldn't avoid. Somehow, she'd have to find the money to cover them. She was too weary to even worry about all that right now. She yawned, politely covering her mouth with her fingers, and then yawned again, not so politely. Her eyes watered and her jaw cracked.

"You're beat." He smiled at her.

"Sorry. I'm not used to digging, I guess."

"I'll go now, so you can get some rest, but I'll be back tomorrow afternoon. The sooner we get the work done, the sooner you can put out the FSBO."

"FSBO?" She vaguely remembered Mae using the term, when Bella had told her she was selling the house herself. Her mother had been against it. Big surprise there. Mae was against almost every decision Bella had ever made—except the decision to marry Gordon. Mae had liked Gordon. Now why hadn't that rung any warning bells?

"FSBO. It's what we smart-alecky real-estate types call 'for sale by owner.'"

"Aren't you going to try and talk me out of that?"

"Nope. Of course, I'll have to commit bodily harm if you ever breathe a word of this to my brother. But I think people have every right to sell their houses themselves."

"Yikes. And after the campaign you waged, who knew? Well, thank you." Bella actually beamed. And then she yawned a third time. "Sorry. I'm not very good company."

He gave her a long, assessing look. "I wouldn't say that. You're honest and you're entertaining. And you make great shipwreck."

"So are puppies and little kids. Honest and entertaining, that is. And I can't cook more than three basic things." She felt absurdly disappointed that he hadn't lied and said she was sexy, or attractive or even cute. Which was ridiculous, because she absolutely didn't care what he thought of her.

"Don't get up—I'll see myself out. Good night, Bella. See you tomorrow."

She took him at his word, because the thought of getting up was close to overwhelming. When she finally made it as far as the kitchen, she found it gleaming.

For the first night since Gordon had left, she slept all the way through until the alarm rang in the morning, and she woke up feeling rested and hungry. She ate cereal and toast and yogurt, and realized she was actually looking forward to the day ahead.

CHAPTER FOUR

BELLA'S SENSE OF well-being lasted until nine-twenty that morning, when the call came from Mr. Nordwick, the principal of Crofton.

After the move from the old neighborhood, Gordon had insisted Josh and Kelsey be enrolled in Crofton House, a private school. Against her better judgment, Bella had agreed. After all, she wanted her kids to have the best education available. She just hadn't been convinced public school wasn't providing it, and she still wasn't certain about Crofton House. The endless stream of BMWs and high-end SUVs dropping off students every morning intimidated her. And Mr. Nordwick had way too much starch in his shorts, she decided now. His tone of voice was both annoyed and condescending.

"Ms. Monroe. As you know, Josh has already been absent once this past week."

Absent? That was news to Bella. Nordwick went on, "And although you wrote a note explaining his absence, I wanted to speak with you."

She hadn't written any note. She opened her mouth to say so, but Nordwick was forging ahead. "He's falling behind and hanging out with boys I consider troublemakers. He'll have to do a lot of extra homework to make certain he stays abreast of his classes. Coincidentally, two of these other young men are also absent today."

Stunned, Bella stammered, "Josh? He—he's not at school? Are you sure?"

"Positive."

Bella said, "I didn't know he was missing school. I had no idea."

Mr. Nordwick's voice changed. "You didn't write a note saying he had to help with the final sale at your store?"

"No, I certainly didn't. I'd never keep him out of school to work at the store. But I know he's at school today, because I dropped him off there an hour ago."

"Well, he must have left again, because he isn't here. That's why I'm calling you. Ms. Monroe, I have an automatic policy that after two absences within a short period of time, a parent is asked to come in and discuss the situation, so if you could come down…"

"I'll do that, Mr. Nordwick, but first I have to find Josh." Bella hung up without saying goodbye. She couldn't seem to catch her breath, and her heart was pounding frantically. There were three customers in the store, and the moment she rang up their purchases and hurried them out, she locked the door and raced to the car.

Where could Josh be? Where would a fifteen-year-old boy go? The city was huge. Where would she begin to look?

Oh, God. What was he up to?

Frightening thoughts of drugs and violence and gangs brought a feeling of panic. Hands trembling on the wheel, Bella drove to the mall where her kids liked to hang out. After three frustrating trips around the lot, she finally found a parking spot and headed inside. Crowds filled the place, and she realized that finding Josh in here was going to be next to impossible.

After forty-five futile minutes, she gave up and went back to her car.

Cursing the traffic, she drove downtown, cruising along the major streets, eyeing the theatre lineups. If he'd already gone into a movie, there was no chance she'd find him. She drove slowly toward the harbor, trying not to imagine him hanging out with street kids, dope dealers, the sad little girls and boys out there selling themselves for money and drugs.

She knew her son was upset over his father's desertion. Who knew how a teenager with raging hormones would handle such a traumatic event? She hated Gordon, truly hated him, for abandoning his children. Surely Josh wouldn't be doing this if his dad hadn't left.

Reason finally penetrated and she turned toward home, still frightened out of her wits. Who could she call? Who would help her find her son? The police? Maybe she should phone the cops. That's what she'd do, she decided, pulling the car into the driveway.

A tiny part of her mind registered that the front of the house looked even worse than before, with fresh sod in clumps and an uneven trench where the sidewalk would be. She couldn't think about that now. She walked past it all, unlocked the front door—and saw Josh's trainers and book bag, dumped on the floor beside the coat closet.

He wasn't in the den. Bella took the stairs two at a time, threw open his bedroom door and choked on a cloud of cigarette smoke. Rap music bombarded her.

Josh and a redheaded boy she didn't recognize were sprawled across his unmade bed. Another boy she'd never seen before was reclining on the carpet. All of them held cigarettes and glasses of what Bella's nose told her was brandy—*her* brandy. Sure enough, the empty bottle sat on the dresser. It had been close to full the last time she had noticed it.

"Josh Monroe, exactly what do you think you're doing?" Bella's voice could be clearly heard, even over the so-called music.

They all leaped to their feet. None of them was too steady. They looked dazed and loose-limbed and foolish.

Josh sported a silly half grin, and his face was flushed. He called over the music, "Hey, Ma, chill, okay? I can explain."

"Turn. That. Noise. Off!"

Josh staggered over to the boom box, punched a button, and silence reigned. One of the boys edged past Bella and hurried down the stairs. The second, the one with red hair, began to gag, and made a headlong dash toward the bathroom. Bella heard the downstairs door slam. Rats and a sinking ship.

A cigarette someone had dropped smoldered on the carpet, and Bella hurried to retrieve it. "Have you taken total leave of your senses, Josh? Look at this carpet, it's got a big burn mark, and it's a miracle you didn't burn the whole house down. And you lied to me, pretending you were at school, when all the time you…you…were playing hooky. It's not the first time, either, is it?"

Words failed her. Realizing she was in serious danger of smacking her son across the ear, she backed away from him.

"Open that window. Clean up this mess. Get that boy in the bathroom *out of here!* And then I want to talk to you, young man."

Feeling sick with both anger and worry, Bella went to the kitchen. She boiled water and made a cup of herbal tea, which was supposed to be calming, but didn't help. In a short while, the red-haired boy came creeping down the stairs, took one hasty look at her and headed out the door.

At last Josh appeared. His face was pale and there was a distinct greenish cast to his skin. He slunk into the kitchen and dropped onto a stool. He kept his head down, not making eye contact.

"How could you, Josh?" Bella's voice was trembling. "I'm having a rough time struggling to keep you in that school, and you're not even attending it. Not only that, you brought strangers into this house, stole my liquor, smoked... Where did you get the cigarettes?"

Josh heaved a beleaguered sigh. "Aww, Ma, stop it. So we skipped out—school's a big yawn, anyway. The cigarettes weren't mine. The guys brought them. And that brandy's been in the cupboard for at least a couple years. It's not as if you were planning to use it anytime soon."

Bella was speechless for a long moment. Then she said, "You get in the car. Now."

He shook his head. "I'm gonna crash for a while. I don't feel so hot."

"Either you get in the car or I'll have Mr. Nordwick drive over here. You're going to tell him exactly what you and your so-called friends were doing."

Josh was looking at her now, his hazel eyes filled with alarm. "Why would I tell old man Nordwick anything? He's a mean old hard-ass.

And I'm not squealing on my friends, so forget that."

"You won't have to. He knows exactly who you were with. And I'm sure he'll give me their names and phone numbers, because I'm calling their parents and telling them exactly what went on here today. On the way to school, you can decide how best to apologize for your actions. There are going to be serious consequences. And there'll be no more foul language around here, either."

"What the hell? I don't care what you do to me," Josh said. "Why don't you just send me to live with Dad? I don't want to be around you, anyway. All you ever talk about is how short we are of money, and how much work there is to do in that damn yard. And if I stick around here, I'll be changing schools all over again next semester— you told me and Kelse you can't afford the fees at Crofton, remember? So what's the difference if I skip out?"

"Go and get in the car." Bella could hear the pain behind his accusations, but this wasn't the time to address it. She had to carry through on her immediate plan.

He slammed the front door behind him, and Bella hurried to the window, afraid he'd bolt. But he was slumped in the car's front seat when she went out. The drive to school was tense.

"I can smell the brandy on you," she told him.

"Yeah, well, I feel like I'm going to barf. And my head hurts."

"That's called a hangover, Josh. And don't even think of being sick in my car."

She had to pull over to the curb after six blocks, while Josh vomited into a storm drain. Everyone on the street gave him a wide berth and stared at Bella.

At the school, Mr. Nordwick was in his office, and the secretary showed them in right away.

Bella explained what had happened, describing the other boys and asking for their names and phone numbers. "I feel their parents should be aware of what they're up to, when they're supposed to be in school."

"I absolutely agree." Nordwick nodded. "I'll be notifying them. My guess would be the boys were Andrew McClain and Ian Carlson. Both are in Josh's homeroom, and they were also absent today without their parents' knowledge. Am I right, Josh?"

Josh didn't respond. He sat with his head down, hands clasped around the arms of the plastic chair.

"Here are their parents' numbers," Nordwick said, handing Bella a slip of paper. "I'll be contacting them myself. Now, as you know, the school has a no-leniency rule when it comes to skipping out. Automatic five-day suspension—you're aware of that, right?"

Bella certainly wasn't. "A five-day suspension? But he's already missed two days, and you're saying he'll be forced to miss five more? Excuse me, but that doesn't make sense."

"It's the rule, and there are no exceptions. Josh can contact his teachers and get assignments for the days he's away. And now if you'll excuse me, I have a meeting and I'm late."

Bella waited in the corridor while Josh gathered assignments from teachers and books from his locker. Classes were ending for the morning, so she located Kelsey's locker and met her there when the lunch bell rang.

Her daughter wasn't exactly delighted to see her. "So, like, what are you doing at school, Mom?"

"Josh and I had to speak to Mr. Nordwick."

"He got caught skipping out, huh? I told him he would."

"Kelsey, if you knew he was doing it, why didn't you tell me?"

Kelsey gave her a horrified look. "Mother, he's my brother."

"Okay. Okay. I understand the loyalty thing, but if you'd told me, things wouldn't have gone this far."

"So, did Josh get suspended?"

"Yes, he did. For five days."

"That is totally whacked. The rules at this school suck."

For the first time in ages, Bella totally agreed her daughter.

"So what's he going to do while you're at work?"

"I haven't decided yet." She ought to be able to trust a fifteen-year-old to stay at home alone, but Josh had just proved he wasn't trustworthy. She'd probably have to bring him to the store with her and give him jobs to do. The thought of dealing with a sullen and resentful teenage boy while trying to remain cheerful for customers made Bella want to scream.

"Can you pick me up when you close the store, Mom? I've got swimming, and it takes forever to get home by bus."

Bella agreed. She drove Josh to the store for the afternoon and gave him work to do. He spent the major portion of the time in the bathroom, however. She heard him vomiting, and had to turn on the radio to keep the sound from the customers.

When closing time finally came, she picked up Kelsey and then drove home. After the turmoil of the day, she'd forgotten that Charlie was coming. The truck was parked in front and she pulled up behind it. Once again, he was wielding a shovel in the front yard.

"You two go and help him," Bella said. "I have to get to the grocery store. There's nothing to eat in the house." She'd forgotten she'd planned to stop on her way home from work.

"Mother." This time Kelsey made it sound like a prayer. "I ruined my nails last night with those *hideous* lumps of dirt, and I absolutely can't do that again. Let me come to the store with you— I'll help pick out groceries and we can figure out what to cook. Please?"

"Okay, Kelsey, but I expect you to work just as hard at making supper as you would hauling dirt. Josh, off *you* go and shovel."

"Can't," he groaned. "I'm sick. I need to lie down."

He did look green. The tender mothering part of her wanted to put a cold cloth on his head and give him Gravol, but Bella hardened her heart. Better that he learned right now about the ravages of alcohol. That was one more thing to worry about.

In a firm tone, she said, "Work will sweat the liquor out of your system. Take your books in the house, change your clothes and then dig."

"Geez, Ma. What's with you, anyhow? You never used to act like this."

"I was never a single parent before. Go."

As if he were heading for the guillotine, Josh made his way to the house. Bella turned off the engine and hurried over to Charlie. She explained about the grocery store and emphasized that Josh was to help with the digging.

"I dropped by the hardware store this morning

with the irrigation guy, but you weren't there," Charlie told her.

"There was... Sorry, I had an emergency."

"Everything okay now?" He sounded as if he really cared, and Bella had the most absurd desire to throw herself against the muscular chest beneath his dirty shirt and cry. Instead, she forced a semblance of a smile.

"It's under control."

"Let me know if there's anything I can do."

"Thanks." She glanced toward the door through which Josh had disappeared. "Just, maybe, if Josh doesn't come out in about ten minutes, would you go and get him? I told him he's to work until dinnertime."

"Absolutely."

"I'll be back soon."

The grocery store was filled with frantic men and women doing exactly what she was doing— shopping after work, trying to keep body and soul together with bread, milk, pasta and hamburger. Except most of them were also buying deli items and frozen dinners, the way Bella had until the money well went dry. She felt sorry for her kids. She couldn't help but feel that Gordon's desertion was somehow her fault, and that Josh and Kelsey were the innocent victims.

"Why don't we make a pot of chili?" Kelsey lifted a tin of kidney beans and waved it at Bella.

"It's good leftover, and we could serve it tonight over garlic mashed potatoes, Auntie Niki made that once when we were over there, and I loved it."

"Good thinking." Bella was amazed by her daughter's ability to come up with a menu. Kelsey must have inherited a long-lost cooking gene from some unknown ancestor. It had never been Bella's favorite activity, and it certainly wasn't Mae's. After Bella's father had left, it was a wonder the two of them hadn't developed scurvy or completely wasted away, since Mae's idea of a nutritional meal was canned soup with crackers.

Kelsey was a huge help, searching out chili powder in one aisle and garlic as Bella located tinned tomatoes and more beans, adding a bag of pre-washed lettuce and some avocado to go in a salad.

"It's lots cheaper if we buy head lettuce and wash it ourselves," Kelsey said, exchanging Bella's package of greens for two large heads of romaine.

"Honey, how do you know all this stuff?"

"We have this *totally* amazing nutrition teacher, Ms. Hargraves? She grew up on a farm, and she explained exactly how she used to have to catch a chicken, chop off its head, pluck the feathers, cut it up and then fry it for dinner. *Yuck!*"

"I agree. I'll have enough trouble cutting up that lettuce."

"Oh, Mom." Kelsey giggled.

Bella had never before heard a word about Ms. Hargraves. Until now, her daughter had answered all questions about school in grunts and monosyllables. In her most fanciful daydreams, Bella had never imagined bonding with her in a grocery store. Perhaps the single positive thing to come out of this entire mess was this new closeness.

"Could we make some chocolate chip cookies, too? There's a recipe for them in that cookbook of yours."

Bella owned exactly one cookbook, a thick copy of *Joy of Cooking* that some kind but misguided soul had given her at a wedding shower.

"Sure, but I don't have a clue what we'll need in the way of ingredients."

"I do." Kelsey recited them, and within moments, flour, baking powder, chocolate chips and oatmeal were loaded in their cart.

Back at the house, Bella was pleased to see that Josh was on his feet and working. Charlie gave them a cheerful wave as she pulled into the garage. Josh studiously looked away.

"Dinner in an hour," she called, as she and Kelsey carried grocery bags into the house. That was probably optimistic, but it sounded positive.

"Great, we're hungry already," Charlie said.

She was making a mistake here, Bella decided. She was beginning to act like the kind of traditional little woman who did for her menfolk, sort of *Little House on the Prairie,* and that wasn't good. It gave them false expectations. Besides which, cooking made her insecure as hell.

"Can we pull this off in an hour, Kelse?"

"Sure. You chop the onions this time, and I'll brown the burger. The rest is just opening cans, right? And I'll mix up the cookies. Did you know you can cook three trays, all at the same time, in our convection oven? Ms. Hargraves says convections are the only way to go."

Who knew? Bella wasn't on intimate terms with her stove. She'd always pretty much relied on the packaged kind of cookie. Wouldn't you know she'd get around to using her high-tech oven about ten minutes before she sold the house? She watched Kelsey bustling around, finding frying pans and mixing bowls, and sadness overwhelmed her. The kid shouldn't get too reliant on their state-of-the-art kitchen, because they'd undoubtedly be moving somewhere with more run-of-the-mill appliances.

If only she could stop obsessing over money. And with every thought about her desperate finances there came a corresponding surge of rage at Gordon, and more disgust for herself. She should have suspected *something.* She'd lived with the damned man for almost seventeen years, so how could she not have recognized how selfish, shallow and dishonest he was? What was wrong with her, to have trusted him? Had she inherited some gene from Mae that simply drove better men away?

And if that was so, why wasn't it working on Charlie?

Irritatingly cheerful, he praised the meal far more than it deserved to be praised—it was only chili, after all.

"I'm going to make it for Daddy when he comes back," Kelsey said, with a sidelong glance at Charlie. "He loves chili."

"Doesn't everybody?" He smiled at her and turned to Bella. "We'll be ready to pour the new sidewalk tomorrow. Do you want me to phone the ready-mix guys?"

"I'll do it." She needed to know how much this was going to cost her.

Charlie nodded. "Tell them to deliver after three. That way I can be here to supervise. They'll just dump the stuff and we'll level it and keep it protected if it rains. Maybe you can give me a hand after school, Josh?"

Bella looked at her son, wondering if he'd admit he was suspended. Josh glanced her way and then hastily muttered something that might have been assent.

Charlie obviously thought so. "That would be a big help," he declared. "I'll come by early in the morning and build the forms. I'm going to need some rough lumber, though."

Bella said, "There's rough lumber at the store. How early do you plan on starting?"

"I thought around five-thirty."

"As in a.m.? That's the middle of the night, Charlie. It's not even light yet. Don't you sleep?"

He avoided her gaze. "Not a lot, no. Three, four hours a night is about my limit."

"That little?" Of course, it was about her limit, too, these days. "Have you always had a sleep disorder?" Before, Bella had normally logged a good seven or eight hours. Maybe they should call each other, keep one another company in the awful night hours. She could play the harmonica for him. All three of her songs. Or there was always phone sex. How did that work, exactly?

"The past few years I've had trouble sleeping." Charlie shook his head and looked uncomfortable, which intrigued Bella. So there were areas of Fredricks's psyche that might not be completely filled with goodness and light. That was comforting, considering the dismal state of her own operating system. Misery did love company.

Predictably, he changed the subject. "Can we pick up the lumber in the morning?"

Bella considered her options and voted for the least painful. "Let's do it right after dinner. Kelsey, you want to serve dessert now?"

The teen blushed with pride as she put a heaping plateful of warm cookies on the table, and the rave reviews she got from Charlie made her beam.

Josh had been silent all during the meal. He'd eaten very little, and he didn't reach for a cookie.

Of course Kelsey noticed. "What? You think I put rat poison in them?"

"They smell awesome, Kelse. I'll try some tomorrow—I just don't feel so good. I think I'll go to bed now."

"But you have to do dishes. Mom, that's *so* not fair. I helped make—"

Bella interrupted, taking pity on both of them. "Okay, Josh, bed. Go do your homework, Kelse. Leave the dishes, and I'll clear up later."

They were gone before the last word was out of her mouth.

Charlie began gathering up silverware. "Let's do it now. You've had a challenging day."

"I have to make a couple phone calls." The parents of the other two boys needed to know what was going on.

"You go ahead, I'll manage here."

But in both cases, she only reached answering machines. Bella left her name and number and asked that each boy's parents call as soon as possible.

When she returned to the kitchen, Charlie had the dishwasher loaded. "Are you always this handy around the house?" she asked. She had never given up trying to get Gordon to share the household chores.

"It comes with being single. I wasn't very good at it when I was married. Guys are basically slobs, and if someone else will do the scut work, we let them."

"How long were you married?" Bella filled the sink and added dish detergent. She and Kelsey seemed to have dirtied every pot and pan in the house.

"Twenty years. Where are the dish towels?"

"Wow. You logged four more years than I did." She opened a drawer and pointed.

He took a towel and reached for the pot she'd just washed. "I don't think we get extra points for time served, do you?"

"Nope. So what happened? Or was it like mine, where you don't know for sure?"

"Oh, I know, all right." He spent more time than necessary wiping a platter. "Five years ago I got involved in a high-speed chase."

Bella turned to look at him. He kept his eyes averted. "This was when you were a cop?"

"Yeah. The guy I was after lost control at an intersection. I couldn't stop, and slammed right into him broadside. I walked away without a scratch, but my partner, Jack, died at the scene. So did the two teenagers who'd stolen the other car."

CHAPTER FIVE

"Wow." Bella stopped washing and turned toward him. "That's terrible. I'm so sorry." It was beyond terrible. It was horrific, and she couldn't imagine the guilt he must feel. Three people dead. She waited, not quite getting the connection, though, as to how it had ended his marriage.

"Jack and I had been partners for a long time. He was my best friend." Charlie swallowed hard and finally met her eyes. His were shadowed.

He said, "I'd always enjoyed a drink, but I started using the stuff to numb all the pain. I got aggressive and unreasonable. I had more than a few complaints lodged about my work. I got into fights in bars."

He dried a pot meticulously, slowly.

"I lost my gun once, which is a very big deal. Found it again, behind a trash can in an alley behind a bar, but the police force suspended me. They sent me for counseling twice, but it didn't take. I got drunk on duty more than a few times, and they finally had to cut me loose."

Bella didn't know what to say. She hadn't pegged him as a drunk. She nodded, waiting.

"My marriage had been shaky for a long time. Alice stuck with me, but I finally had the good sense to pack my bags and leave. I wasn't a nice person to be around. My daughter, Emma, blamed me—rightly so—and wouldn't speak to me for a long time. That was probably the lowest point of my life."

Bella busied herself with the dishes. "So you pretty much lost everything." They had a lot in common.

"Yeah. Rock bottom. Funny how that's what it takes sometimes to make a guy wake up. I joined AA, and when I'd been sober six months, my brother offered me a job if I got my real-estate license. Offered to pay for the course. I was beyond broke by that time, so I swallowed my pride and accepted."

She'd figured Rick Fredricks for a class-A jerk, but this showed him in a somewhat different light. "Good brother. I always wished I'd had one of those."

"You an only child?"

"Yup." Bella pulled the plug and rinsed out the sink. "We're done here. Let's go get the lumber."

They were in the truck, driving down Oak Street, when he said, "Josh is looking pretty rough. I hope he's not getting the flu?"

Bella snorted. "Not likely." She might as well tell him, since he'd find out anyway. "He and two friends cut classes today, holed up in my house, drank the last of my brandy and smoked enough cigarettes to give themselves lung cancer. He's been suspended from school for a week. He's hungover, is his problem. I figured some hard physical labor wouldn't hurt, and then maybe he'll think twice next time before guzzling a bottle of brandy." She took a shaky breath and added, "I didn't know what else to do. He's only fifteen, and he needs an education. I'm so scared for Josh—he's really acting out since his father left."

Without any warning, she started to cry, and hard as she tried, she couldn't stop. The worry she felt for her kids was overwhelming.

Charlie pulled the truck over into a bus stop, fished in the glove box and handed her a packet of tissues. Then he gathered her into his arms and held her close, gently patting her back.

Bella gasped and snuffled and snorted, blotted her streaming eyes, made a superhuman effort to stop the sobs and failed dismally.

"Shoot. I'm sorry," she wailed, hating herself for being so transparent.

"Just let 'er rip," Charlie advised. Her head was on his chest, and his voice sounded deep and comforting. "It's the best way to get through it."

She couldn't do anything else. Finally, after

what seemed an embarrassingly long time, she blew her nose again and the tears slowed and then stopped. She was exhausted. Feeling empty and strangely light, as well as muddleheaded, she let herself rest on his shoulder.

"Sorry," she finally repeated, sitting up straighter. "Thanks."

He kept his arm around her. "I always liked these bench seats in trucks," he said. "They're way friendlier than bucket seats."

She nodded. Her nose was stuffed, and talking was an effort. Trying to think of what to say was also an effort, so she kept quiet.

"You want a coffee? There's a Starbucks on the next block."

"Yes, please." Her throat was dry and her eyes were sore. She'd probably looked a mess before, but now she'd frighten little children.

He started the truck with one arm still around her. She wondered if she ought to move away, and decided it was way too much effort. To hell with the seat belt—surely nothing could happen in one city block. Although with her luck lately, and the way his arm made her feel…

She moved over and fastened the belt.

At the coffeehouse, she didn't want to go in. Who needed to advertise she'd had a meltdown? He brought her out a large latte, with cream and caramel sauce.

Parked on the busy street, they sipped their coffees quietly, but the silence was companionable. Bella found it restful, being with him. Unless she got too close.

"You said Josh was suspended. Is that going to be a problem, leaving him alone during the day?"

"I'm taking him to the store—it's the only way I can be sure he stays out of trouble. He's not going to be very happy about it, though, because he's always hated being there."

After a moment, Charlie said, "I'll be working in your garden most afternoons, starting about two or three. I can drop by and pick him up, if you like. If it's raining, I'll start on the powder room and the kitchen. If you don't mind? I could really use his help."

Mind? It was like a gift from God.

"That would be fantastic. If he'll even go with you. You must have noticed he's been pretty rebellious since Gordon left."

"Understandable. My brother and I grew up without a father, and it's not easy." Charlie finished his coffee and crumpled the cup, shoving it into a paper bag.

"So did I." The coincidence was surprising. "Mine left with another woman. What happened to yours?"

"He was killed. He worked on the docks as a longshoreman and there was an accident. He and my mother weren't ever legally married, so there was no pension or anything."

"How old were you?"

"Two. Rick was four. Of course, neither of us remembers him at all. But Mom's showed us pictures."

"That must have been tough for her, left to raise two little boys. I know it was for my mother, and I was fifteen when my dad left." Bella thought about it and shook her head. "I honestly don't know how our mothers did it. It looks like it'll be impossible for me to ever earn enough to support my kids, never mind put away enough for them to go to college."

Mae, Charlie's mother and now her, all left to raise children alone, with no support. Bella wondered how many other women there were in similar straits. At least it made her feel less alone, knowing she wasn't the only one. She finished her coffee, lingering over the caramel in the bottom of the cup.

Charlie started the truck and pulled into traffic. "College was out of the question for Rick and me."

"For me, too. I did manage two semesters at art school, though. I worked for College Pro painters to earn enough for tuition."

"So that's how you got so good with a paint-brush. What were you studying at art school?"

"General courses. I thought I might try interior design. But then I met Gordon. He was in university, working on a degree in accounting. We got married, and it made more sense for me to work full-time, so he could finish school. I got a job with the original owners of the hardware store. When he graduated, Gordon had more earning potential than I did. The agreement was that when he was done I'd go back to design school, but I'd gotten pregnant by then. I had Josh, and then Kelsey came along."

"How did you end up buying the store?"

"I went on working weekends, selling paint and advising people on colors. The owners were getting old and eventually they decided to sell. Gordon worked for an accounting firm, but he hated it. He wanted a business of his own, so buying the hardware store seemed a good idea. And it was, at least at first. We changed the name to Monroe's and worked super hard building up the business. You don't get rich running a small neighborhood store, but we made a good living until that lousy big-box store opened six months ago. Then things went downhill fast."

Charlie drove to Monroe's and Bella led him out back, where the lumber was. She'd sold off a fair amount already, but there was still a lot left.

"What are you going to do with the stock that's left over, when you close for good?"

"I'm not sure." It was one of the questions she'd spent her sleepless hours pondering. "The suppliers won't take it back, and I'll have to pay them. I don't have anywhere to store it. I'll probably end up practically giving it to one of the clearance houses."

"Don't be too hasty. We can use a fair amount on renovations, and you can bill me for it as the houses sell. I know a guy with a big empty garage and maybe he'd warehouse it for you."

"You seem to know a lot of helpful people."

"Yeah, I meet most of them at AA."

"I never thought of AA as a resource center."

"Neither did I, but it's turned out to be one. Like I said before, we never know what anything is for."

Was that true? Bella wondered as they loaded the wood into the truck. It seemed to call for a child-like trust that she found impossible to imagine.

When the lumber for the sidewalk was safely stowed in the shed behind the house, Charlie shut the door and fastened the padlock. "I'll head home now, but I'll be back early."

"There'll be coffee ready." It would be good to have another adult around in the early morning hours.

"Night, Bella." It seemed perfectly natural when he leaned in close and pressed a kiss on her cheek. It would have been only a friendly gesture if she hadn't turned her head, so their lips connected.

The kiss was clumsy at first, but then they got the hang of it. His arms came around her and pulled her in close, and hers slid around his neck.

It had been a long time since she'd been kissed with passion. Actually, it had been a long time since she'd been kissed at all. Charlie knew his way around a woman's mouth, and she gave herself up to the pleasure.

He was the one who broke it off, but gently. He held her close for another long moment and then stepped back. He stroked a hand slowly over her hair and down the side of her face. She couldn't really see him clearly, since the night sky was overcast. Her lips throbbed, and secret parts of her that had been sleeping for quite a while woke up and demanded more.

"Night, Bella," he repeated. "See you tomorrow."

Feeling shell-shocked and uncomfortably aroused, she watched him walk to the pickup. He turned and gave her a single wave before he climbed in, and she came to her senses and hurried into the house, wondering what had possessed her. Whatever it was, she needed to get over it. She had enough complications in her life without adding an impoverished recovering alcoholic, regardless of how hungry he made her feel.

CHAPTER SIX

KISSING HER HADN'T BEEN the smartest thing he'd ever done, but it sure as hell had felt good. When the door closed behind Bella, Charlie started the truck, but before he drove away he checked his cell phone. He'd had it turned off, and yet he knew Alice would have called at least five times. There were actually six calls. He clicked for messages, and sighed as he listened to her soft but insistent voice.

"Charlie, I can't figure out how to work the new alarm system, could you come by and show me?"

"Charlie, I'm scared to go to bed without the alarm set—I called Emma but the batteries must be out on her cell. Could you please come by and do this for me?"

"Charlie, I've called and called. Surely it's not too much to ask you to just drop by for a few minutes?"

"Charlie, I finally got hold of Emma, but she has

an exam tomorrow. She said to call you again, and that if you couldn't come and fix this for me, she'd drive over. But I don't want to disturb her, she needs her sleep. I wish you'd answer your phone, Charlie. It's rude not to answer me. And it's hard on Emma."

He cancelled the remaining two calls without listening, knowing they'd be more of the same. With a sigh, he headed for his ex-wife's house, knowing she'd have every light on, knowing the exact tone of voice she'd use to remind him she hadn't been able to go to bed, just because of him.

He was sure there were probably psychological explanations for Alice's constant demands. He knew she was controlling and insecure and dangerously dependent. He knew he'd have to do something about it sooner or later. He just didn't know what to do or how to do it.

He thought of Bella, as he was doing more often these days.

He'd been deliberately encouraging her to depend on him, hoping that she'd cave and give him the listing. If that happened, he'd make sure she got top dollar when the time came to sell her house. It was devious, but the arrangement worked for both of them, didn't it?

The only drawback was he was getting involved with her a little deeper than he'd planned. The kids, too. It was becoming complicated.

The other drawback was that she didn't know about the thousand-dollar bonus Rick had offered, or the side bets his brother had made with the guys at the office. To Rick, Bella Monroe had become a challenge.

But if Charlie got the listing, he wasn't cheating her out of anything. In fact, she was going to benefit. She'd get a cut on commission, if they managed to improve the no-sells enough to move them. He was adding thousands to the price of her house with the improvements. And he'd contacted Barney Kalamis, his friend down at the station. Barney worked in missing persons and he was doing some digging into Gordon Monroe's vanishing act.

It was all fair and aboveboard. All except wanting to get Bella naked. Charlie really had to put that out of his mind. This was a business deal, and it was never a good idea to mix business and pleasure.

BELLA MADE A POT of coffee early the next morning and left the door unlocked. She had a quick shower and got dressed to the sound of hammering, and by the time she made it out to the front yard, Charlie was well along with the forms. To her amazement, Josh was working alongside him, neatly fitting pieces of two-by-four into the sides of the six-inch-deep trench they'd made for the sidewalk. She hadn't even heard her son get up.

"Thanks for the coffee." Charlie gave her a big

smile, and Bella returned it, feeling shy about last night's kissing session.

"Want a refill?"

"In a bit. We'll soon be done here. It's gone fast, because Josh is helping."

"Couldn't sleep," Josh mumbled, as if he was doing something wrong. "Went to bed way early. Could I have some hot chocolate?"

Bella felt proud of him. The poor kid had to be hungover, but here he was, working the dawn away. She ruffled his hair and said, "Absolutely. Coming right up. And how about breakfast? I can probably manage toast and scrambled eggs for the two of you." What was happening to her? She was turning into Nigella, or whatever that English cooking goddess's name was.

"Breakfast sounds fantastic." Charlie went back to sawing lengths of wood, handing them off to Josh.

Bella hurried inside, shivering. She made Josh his hot chocolate and took it out, then poured herself some coffee, taking it into the study, where the computer was. She turned it on and called up her banking information, but there hadn't been any miracles since yesterday. Her account was basically running on empty, and the ready-mix people had asked for a check on delivery, which meant she needed eight hundred dollars by this afternoon.

It might as well have been a million. She

couldn't see where the money was going to come from, unless the store did an amazing amount of business today. And pigs took to the sky.

With the now familiar ache in her gut over money, she shut down her computer. If worst came to worst—and it seemed inevitable that it would—she was going to have to go against every instinct and borrow from Mae. But Bella was determined to wait until absolutely the last moment before she gave in and asked, knowing the interest, in the form of emotional payback, was sure to be expensive.

As if she'd conjured her up, Bella's mother walked into the store just before noon. Tiny and impeccably coiffed, Mae was wearing a mauve pantsuit under a red raincoat. She waved at Bella, who was standing on a ladder retrieving stock from a high shelf. Then she turned her attention to her grandson.

"Josh, honey, what are you doing here? Shouldn't you be in school?"

"I got suspended," he said in a loud voice. He knew if he mumbled his grandmother would just go on asking until she got it straight.

"Suspended? Is that the same as expelled?" She sounded horrified, as well she might, Bella thought. Her mother's hand was doing its pat-pat thing over her heart, the gesture that always indicated stress.

"It means I can't go back to school for a week, Gran."

"Oh, Josh. Oh my goodness. What on earth did you do?"

"I skipped out."

"You played hooky? Well, you're probably missing your father—it's bound to cause you emotional problems." Mae turned her attention to Bella.

"Didn't you go to the school and explain that the children are having a rough time just now, Annabella?" Her mother was the only living person who ever called Bella by her full birth name. "It's better to be open about these kinds of things," she added. "It makes it hard on Kelsey and Josh for you to be so secretive about Gordon leaving. I went to the school immediately when your father ran off, and I had a talk with all your teachers. You should have done the same, Annabella."

Two minutes, and Mae had found a new way to make it all her fault, Bella thought, finally finding the packages of electrical outlets she'd known had to be there somewhere. It probably *was* her fault, but it didn't make her feel any better to be reminded. She climbed down the ladder and handed the packages to Josh.

"Put these out for me. That man in the peaked cap said he'd be back for them." She tried her surest formula for getting her mother off her back.

"How are you, Mom? Are your teeth feeling any better?"

Mae, who'd enjoyed years of supposed ill health, had somehow convinced a hapless dentist to extract her teeth and fit her with dentures. Which so far had provided her with months of delicious complaining.

"They're making me another new set—that's the third now. I threatened to sue that dentist, although that snob of a Sidney Richfield wouldn't do a thing to help me. I told Ruth she ought to speak to him. He needs taking down a peg or two."

During Bella's teen years, Sidney's mother, Ruth, and Mae had tried their best to instigate a romance between their children. It hadn't worked, only partly because Sidney was gay. He'd also been supercilious and snide. He was now a lawyer with his own firm, and he hadn't changed at all.

At Mae's suggestion, Bella had called Sidney two days after Gordon left, to ask his advice. He'd told her in a frosty tone that he only did corporate law, and that she should contact a divorce lawyer.

Which would have been perfectly fine if she had any money.

Mae was saying, "I had to use Harriet's cousin's sister—she's a lawyer, too. You should maybe call her, because I think you're being too hasty selling this business, Annabella. How are you going to support the children? It's not as if you have a career to fall back on."

Now, why hadn't Bella thought of that?

"There just isn't enough business to stay open, Mom. And without sales, I can't afford the lease."

"You need to be patient, dear. Business will pick up, there's always highs and lows—there was when I worked at Sears."

Bella figured Sears probably was a teensy bit more solid financially than she was. "It's been six months now, Mom, and things haven't improved. Sales have gone downhill steadily, and I'm flat out of money. I told you Gordon took everything we had, even the damned Volvo."

The lease payments of which Bella was liable for. Sidney had clarified that much, at least.

"Read the fine print on the lease, honey," he'd said in his nasal voice. "I expect you'll find that if you both signed, in the event of one or the other of you dying or leaving, the other one is fully responsible. Lease contracts are binding. You're still legally married, I take it?"

"Yes." Bella had tried not to panic, but it was a losing battle.

"Then I would say you're going to have to pay. Unless he does. How do you know he won't?"

She knew. Gordon had said in return for the Volvo and their savings he was signing over the business and the house to her. She was getting the whopping mortgage, the failing business, the lease on the car, and the kids, while he drove away in the Volvo with all their money. What a deal.

And now Mae was pushing every button Bella had.

"But what are you going to do?" her mom nagged. "You'll have to find a job. Maybe you can get one at Sears."

Not in this lifetime. Not that there was anything wrong with working for a department store, but the thought of following in her mother's footsteps was Bella's worst nightmare.

It was all she could do to hold her tongue now. She took several deep breaths, and then said, "Mom, I have to close this store, dispose of the inventory and then sell the house." She wasn't about to mention Charlie or his shotgun houses. The round of questions about that would take the rest of the day and most of the night. "I just don't have time or energy to work anywhere else at the moment. When the time comes, I'll think about it."

And then Mae made her feel ashamed of her bad temper. "I understand, dear," she said. "In the meantime, let me help you out, Annabella. I have that five thousand put away—the money's just sitting doing nothing, and you might as well use it."

Bella was humbled by her mother's generosity. The "five thousand" was all Mae had in the world,

besides her cozy little unit at Ocean Acres, the re-
tirement community where she'd lived for the past
five years.

It was terrible to have to accept, but Bella really
had no other choice.

The cement truck was probably already on its
way. The driver had kindly offered to stop at
Monroe's to pick up the payment, and she didn't
have anywhere close to eight hundred dollars. Last
time she'd looked, she had $89.98 in the till and
another eighteen dollars in her wallet.

Promising Mae she'd pay her back as soon as
she possibly could, Bella swallowed her pride and
thanked her mother for the check.

NOW THAT PAYING FOR THE concrete wasn't a problem, it was exciting to see the new sidewalk when
she got home. True to his word, Charlie had come
by and picked up Josh at three. Her son had been
so relieved to be sprung from the store that he
actually greeted Charlie with, "Hey, man, how's
it goin'?"

Even without anything planted, the front garden looked much improved, and the winding sidewalk lent an air of graciousness to the property.
Bella felt her spirits lift. Maybe somehow things
would improve.

Kelsey came running into the garage to greet
her, and Bella's heart gave a joyful thump. Being

on better terms with her daughter was almost worth everything.

Almost.

"Guess what, Mom? Charlie let me put coins in the cement. He says it's good luck—something about abundance."

"How many?"

"Seven dollars. It's what our house numbers add up to—124 added together."

"Let's hope he's right."

"Can we make tuna casserole for dinner? Ms. Hargraves taught us how to do it in class today."

"Do we have any tuna?"

"Sure. Don't you remember we bought two cans at the grocery yesterday?"

All Bella remembered about the grocery store was praying hard that her debit card would cover what they were buying. At least Mae's money would float them for another few weeks. By that time, the house would have hit the market, and with luck it would sell fast. Bella couldn't bear to think about what she'd do if it sat unsold for any length of time.

And Christmas was coming. Mae would make sure the kids had gifts, but Bella wanted so much to be able to get them things herself.

Money doesn't buy happiness, Mae always said.

But Bella figured it could go a long way toward producing a little peace of mind.

CHAPTER SEVEN

ELEVEN DAYS LATER, at five-forty-five in the afternoon, Bella and Kelsey watched as Charlie hammered a wooden frame into the bark mulch that outlined the newly planted beds in the front garden.

Josh hung the neatly lettered For Sale By Owner sign on it. They'd all worked since dawn, Charlie and Josh finishing the planting and Bella and Kelsey trying to make the inside look less lived-in, just in case a prospective buyer turned up immediately.

Holding an umbrella to keep the rain off her head, Bella said, "The sign looks classy, don't you think?"

"I think so," Charlie agreed. "But then, Josh and I made it, so maybe we're a little prejudiced."

Bella shook her head. "Nope, it looks really professional. Let's hope it attracts someone wonderful who wants to buy this place. Preferably this afternoon. Tomorrow, at the very latest."

Charlie laughed, but Bella couldn't see the humor.

Mae's money was disappearing rapidly. Charlie had used materials from the hardware store and things he'd scrounged from God-knew-where, but still there had been an alarming quantity of stuff Bella had had to buy: plumbing fixtures for the downstairs bathroom, plants and shrubs for the garden. And there were the mortgage payments, utilities, groceries, school fees—the list seemed to multiply daily. Most infuriating of all was the hefty lease payment on the missing Volvo. She'd cursed Gordon all over again when she saw the automatic debit from the account.

"It's going to sell right away. This is a day to celebrate," Charlie declared. "How about I take everyone out for dinner? That is, if we can use your car, Bella? We won't fit in the truck."

"Yes." Josh punched one fist into the other palm.

"Excellent." Kelsey jumped up and down.

Bella knew the kids were eager, but she hesitated. Ever since what she labeled as "the kissing incident," she'd been careful not to be alone with Charlie. But she couldn't very well refuse this invitation.

Because of their finances, they hadn't eaten out once since Gordon left. She couldn't very well deny Josh and Kelsey this treat. Josh had worked hard, and thanks to Kelsey's input there'd been some sort of home-cooked meal every night. There'd also been a couple of colossal failures, but what the heck. Eight out of ten wasn't bad.

And it wasn't as if this was a date. Bella needed to get a grip. The kids would be right there. It was simply a friendly gesture on Charlie's part.

"Thank you," she said. "Of course we'll take the car. Are we okay, casual?"

"My tux is at the cleaners, so I guess we'll have to go as we are."

Bella tossed her keys to him. "You drive, Charlie. I'll just grab a different jacket—this one's wet."

He headed toward the garage. "Climb in the limo, guys."

Bella trotted into the house. She did need a dry jacket, but she also wanted to check out the new haircut Niki had given her two days before, her belated birthday present.

She still wasn't used to it, and she wasn't sure if she liked it. It was more a brush cut than a hairdo, and Niki had told her it was meant to stand on end at all times, but the change had been a shock.

"Yikes. I look like I've just stuck my finger in a light socket," Bella had gasped.

"Now you're interesting and modern, instead of your usual predictable, frumpy and downtrodden self," Niki had pronounced, as sensitive as a plank. "So have you done the nasty deed with sexy Charlie yet?"

Bella could feel the other four clients in the shop snap to attention. Niki had a voice that carried.

"Niki. For Pete's sake."

"Who's Pete? Hasn't Charlie come on to you? Hell, maybe he's gay after all. But he sure didn't seem like he was."

"He's not gay. He's kind of… Sort of…" She dropped her voice to a whisper. "Sexy. He kissed me a couple times."

"Well, hey, girl, high five. Way to go. Give him some encouragement, why don't you?"

"I'm still married. It bothers me—it feels like I'm cheating."

"On who? The jerk who waltzed off with all your money and the car? You don't owe him a damn thing, honey. Ask yourself, if he appeared at the door tomorrow, would you take him back?"

Bella had given that a lot of thought. "No. I want a divorce."

"And you'll get one, when you find him. Go see my uncle Niko, the one I was named after. He's a notary and he'll get the right papers together for you—he does it for everyone in the family. I'll call him and tell him to expect you." She rubbed something that looked like axle grease into what was left of Bella's hair. "In the meantime, you're going to forget how to have sex, and we don't want that, do we? Remember how much there was to figure out the first time?"

Bella thought about that as she rubbed some of the goop Niki had given her on her hands now, and smoothed it through her hair, restoring the electric shock effect. She used eyeliner and her eyelash curler, and daubed some gloss on her mouth.

A little bit of powder, a little bit of paint. Makes a little lady look like what she ain't. Mae's favorite rhyme for applying makeup.

How, exactly, should she go about encouraging Charlie, anyhow? The few sexual partners she'd had in her life hadn't seemed to need much encouragement. Maybe there was an idiot's guide to middle-aged dating. Maybe she could swap her guide to living well for that? Not that she was dating, she reminded herself.

She found a faded denim jacket and headed out.

Josh and Kelsey were already in the backseat.

Bella got into the front. Johnny Cash was on the sound system, growling about Folsom Prison. Bella told herself to try some of his songs on the harmonica.

Charlie started the car and gave her an assessing look.

"I wasn't sure at first, but now I like your hair that way," he said.

"See, Mom, I told you it's hot," Kelsey confirmed, and then spoiled it by adding, "Dad's going to love it."

"Where are we going to eat?" Josh asked. His mother's hair was way down on his priority list.

Charlie said, "How about Hamburger in Paradise? My daughter likes it there, and there's lots besides burgers."

Enthusiastic agreement came from the backseat. Charlie raised an inquiring eyebrow at Bella.

"Anywhere with a menu's fine by me." She was tired of the unrelenting daily pressure to come up with meals.

The restaurant was obviously a current spot for young people. There was a ten-minute wait for a table, but once they were served, the food was great.

Charlie ordered a bottle of wine, and Bella was enjoying a glass with her Caesar salad when a sharp female voice exclaimed, "I thought you said you were working tonight, Dad."

The young woman's long-lashed green eyes flicked over Bella, slid past Josh and Kelsey and then homed in on Charlie. She looked and sounded anything but friendly. She was pretty, and her long, curly auburn hair was pulled back, emphasizing high cheekbones and tilted eyes. Charlie's gray-green eyes. She was very angry.

"Emma. I had no idea you were here." He shot to his feet and put an arm around her shoulders.

"Honey, I want you to meet Bella Monroe. Bella, this is my daughter, Emma. And these are Bella's kids, Kelsey and Josh."

"Hi, Emma." Bella smiled up at her. "It's a pleasure to meet you."

Emma didn't look at all pleased to meet them. In fact, she looked murderous.

"Hi," she said briefly, turning back to her father as if the others were invisible. In an accusing voice, she said, "You know Mom needs that dresser moved, Dad. And there's some problem with the upstairs bathroom. She was expecting you over there this evening."

"I'll be there a little later." Charlie didn't sound perturbed, but Bella noticed that the hand not on Emma's shoulder had clenched into a fist. "Come and join us, why don't you?"

"No thanks, I'm with friends." Emma gestured vaguely toward a table in the back. "Nice to meet you," she said in Bella's general direction as she stalked off.

Charlie, looking flushed, sat back down. For the rest of the meal he maintained a cheerful conversation, talking about the food, urging everyone to have dessert, making a funny story out of mishaps he and Josh had encountered constructing the sign. But his glance went often to the table where his daughter sat. Her back was turned to them, and Bella noticed Emma didn't once look around.

Charlie paid the bill, and before they left he made his way to his daughter's table, bending over to say something to her.

Curious, Bella watched. Emma didn't get up. She shrugged elaborately, and it was obvious she didn't introduce him to any of her friends. But then, maybe he already knew them all.

Charlie leaned closer and said something else to her, and then he straightened, turned and led Bella and the kids out of the restaurant.

Bella knew, all too well, what it was like to have children who were rude and blamed one parent for all the problems in a marriage. Although Josh hadn't skipped school again and had been good lately about working with Charlie, he wasn't exactly supportive.

He'd been furious when she'd finally made contact with Andrew's and Ian's parents. The other boys had also been suspended, but she hadn't told Josh that the McClains and the Carlsons had pretty much laughed the whole thing off. Regis Carlson had actually said, "Boys will be boys." And when Bella pointed out that boys became men all too soon, he'd become haughty and reminded her he was on the board of trustees at Crofton.

"I went there myself, and we got up to mischief in my time, as well—it's perfectly natural. If there's any damage to your house, send me the bill."

Carlson's attitude had left Bella convinced that the sooner her kids were back in public school, the better.

The times she'd tried to talk to Josh about his father's disappearance, he'd refused to discuss it. Bella wondered if Josh, like his sister, honestly believed she'd driven Gordon away.

So watching Charlie with his daughter was comforting, in a way. It was reassuring to know that other parents had problems with their children, too. On the other hand, she felt sorry for Charlie.

When he pulled up in front of their house, Josh and Kelsey thanked him and then bailed out of the car. He'd left the motor running, meaning to return the car to the garage, and Bella was about to get out when he reached across and touched her arm.

"Can we talk for a minute?"

"Sure." She'd already opened the car door, and she closed it again and settled back in the seat.

He turned the motor off. "I wanted to apologize for Emma's behavior," he began.

Bella shook her head and put a hand on his wrist. "No need," she said. "Remember how awful Josh was to you at first? Young people can be pretty self-centered, and they don't even realize half the time that they're being rude."

"She's loyal to her mother. She thinks the divorce was my fault, and she's been trying to get us back together."

"Oh." Bella thought that over. "How probable is that?"

"About the same as world peace happening before midnight. Alice and I married because Emma was on the way, the consequence of a one-night stand after a party. I knew from the start I didn't love her, but I didn't want any kid of mine growing up without a father."

"Yeah. I know that feeling. It's one of the reasons I stayed with Gordon even after I was pretty sure I didn't love him anymore." She'd been thinking a lot about that. Gordon must have guessed. Maybe she should have just come out and said it. Maybe if she had, they could have come to some arrangement that didn't involve him walking out and leaving his children.

"Staying because of the kids." She sighed. "I guess it's the oldest reason in the world for hanging on in a marriage that doesn't work."

"Yeah, but I can't very well tell my daughter I stayed with her mother because of her." Charlie sounded angry. "It puts way too much responsibility in the wrong place. But when you don't tell them some version of the truth, things get really screwed up." He smacked one palm against the steering wheel. "See, Emma's got it cemented into her head that we can get together again, Alice and I."

Just like Kelsey. "And I guess Emma probably

figured there was something between the two of us, having dinner with the kids and everything."

"Yeah. That's pretty much dead-on."

"Hasn't she seen… I mean, haven't you…" Bella felt her face getting hot. "Don't you take women out, Charlie?"

"As in dating?" He gave a harsh laugh. "Not really. I've been pretty busy this past couple of years, getting sober, taking that real-estate course… My God, I thought the exams for the police force were tough, but they were a cinch compared to that. Lots of math, most of which I'd forgotten since high school. And then after I squeaked through, it finally dawned on me that it maybe wasn't exactly the job I was born to do."

"But women must come on to you." Bella's face grew even hotter. She'd certainly given it a good deal of thought.

"Oh, yeah, the odd one. There's a woman at the office, Janice Feldergast." He caught himself. "But attraction has to be a mutual thing, and usually it hasn't been."

Bella couldn't help but wonder where that left her.

To get them off such dangerous ground, she said, "If you had your dream job, what would it be?"

"I'm not sure. I'm not good at selling, and that's becoming obvious. I'd like more physical stuff— gardening, fixing things."

"From what I've seen, you're a master handy-man. Do up a résumé, and I'll write you a glowing recommendation."

He really had a great smile. And he really had a great mouth. She turned away, pretending to be interested in a car driving past.

"Thanks, Bella. For understanding about Emma."

"Hey, I've got teenagers. It goes with the territory."

"I've got some news about your husband, by the way."

"You do?"

"It's not much, no definite location yet, but he crossed the border at Tijuana three days after he left Vancouver. He was driving the Volvo, said he was heading down the coast. Which leaves a lot of territory to cover, but my friend Barney has contacts all over the place. He'll locate him sooner or later."

"I don't know how to thank you."

"Think paint. Think backbreaking work on those houses."

She was thinking something entirely different, and she was glad it was dark in the car. Flustered, she reached for the door handle.

"I really enjoyed my dinner. Thanks for taking us."

"My pleasure. We'll do it again sometime soon." He was looking straight at her. "Maybe just the two of us next time?"

"As in…dating?"

He laughed at the pretended horror in her tone. "Is that such a bad idea?"

"I dunno. It *is* a scary thought, Charlie. I haven't dated in sixteen years. And even then I wasn't much good at it. Figuring out what to wear, what to talk about, whether or not there was food stuck in my teeth."

He leaned closer, staring at her mouth. "Actually, I was going to mention that food thing."

Bella's hand shot up.

"I'm teasing. You're way too serious. Your teeth are fine. In fact, I've noticed you have really excellent teeth." He laughed again, and then reached over and gently took her hand away. His voice was a low murmur. "And even with food stuck in them, you'd be a knockout."

She had the urge to look over her shoulder, see who he was talking to. It certainly couldn't be her.

"I…" She remembered a rule she'd heard long ago, maybe on *Oprah*. It wasn't Mae this time, she was sure of that.

When someone pays you a compliment, just say thank-you.

"Thank you." Her voice was high and breathy. She knew she should stop there, but she couldn't. "I've never thought of myself like that."

"Well, start. Because you're lovely. That's what Bella means, doesn't it? Beautiful?"

"It's just a nickname for Annabella. My father had relatives in Italy." This was getting way too intimate. "I should go in now." She reached again for the door opener.

Charlie put out a hand to detain her, and for an instant, she thought he was going to kiss her. She hoped he was.

Instead, he said, "We should start soon on the other houses. When can you spare some time to come with me and look at them?"

Okay. Business, Bella. Get that through your skull; this is really just business.

"I have to be packed up and out of the store by Wednesday morning—they gave me a couple extra days. As soon as I'm finished there, I'll have time. There isn't much left to clean up, thanks to you." He'd found space in an empty building and, with the use of the pickup, they'd transferred almost all the unsold stock.

"Good. I have to go to a meeting tomorrow afternoon—Rick has these meetings every so often to buoy up the troops. But it should be finished by three. I'll come by after that and give you a hand cleaning up." He started the car and drove into the garage. It was dark in there, and she could barely see him.

"Charlie, you've already done so much. I can finish the rest."

"Yeah, well, the sooner the store is cleaned

out, the sooner we can get going on those properties, right?"

Funny how darkness made her so aware of his voice, deep and resonant.

He sighed. "The other salespeople have bets going, that I'll never move even one. I'm determined to sell all three. And like I promised, I'll give you a cut on the commission if you can figure out how to improve them."

"Can we start on Wednesday at noon, then?" It wasn't as if anyone else was lining up to offer her a job. And a cut on the commission was an excellent incentive. She thought of asking how much of a cut, but she didn't. Surely by now she could trust him?

"Okay." He leaned over without touching her and pressed his lips to hers, but only briefly.

The degree to which she wanted more sent her scuttling out of the car. She opened the door and blinked at how bright it seemed outside.

"See you Wednesday," he said, getting out. "Here are your keys. We'll drive my BMW next time, I promise."

She took the keys and headed for the house, barely noticing the older man walking slowly past the front of the property. She was hanging up her jacket in the front hall, thinking about that almost kiss, when the doorbell rang. Figuring Charlie had forgotten something, she pulled it open with a smile.

It was the man who'd been walking along the sidewalk a minute earlier. Her first thought was, *This is amazing, he's come to buy the house.*

But when she took a good look at him, he seemed familiar.

He stood, hat in one hand, looking at her and not saying anything. Then he reached up and smoothed a few strands of gray hair across a bald spot, and Bella suddenly felt a strange tightness in her chest.

"Bella mia? Don't you remember me?"

It was the voice that did it, that gravelly smoker's rasp that was part of her earliest memory—that, and the pet name. Only one person had ever called her *Bella mia.*

"Dad?" Her mouth fell open. She could feel herself beginning to tremble. Years melted away, and she was fifteen again.

"Daddy?"

It couldn't be. And yet…

CHAPTER EIGHT

HE NODDED. "Yeah, honey. It's me. My God, you look so good."

She saw the tears in his hazel eyes, but all she could think of were the endless, lonely hours she'd imagined this very scenario when she was growing up. And the fact that it had never happened, despite her prayers. She remembered the bargains she'd made with God.

Bring him back, and I'll never smoke again. I'll stop swearing, I won't let Billy Wilson feel me up.

"Could I maybe come in?" His tone was humble, the look in his eyes beseeching. "Please, *Bella mia,* I would really like to talk to you."

"It's just Bella." She put as much ice in her tone as she could manage. Reluctantly, she stood aside so he could come through the door. It was only out of curiosity, she told herself. She simply wanted to know what he was doing here, after all this time.

"You must wonder why I'm here."

"Yeah, I guess I do, Not that it really matters. I mean, why bother coming back now? After all these years?"

His face was thinner. Deep lines made grooves around his eyes and mouth. "Dinah passed away a couple weeks ago." His eyes filled with tears. "She got sick soon after we left Vancouver. She had multiple sclerosis. Traveling was hard on her."

Dinah Flynn. Bella really couldn't find it in her heart to be compassionate about the woman her father had run away with—the woman who'd stolen him away from Mae, and from Bella.

"And I suppose you had a permanently disabled arm so you couldn't write, is that it?" Bella could feel tremors going through her, waves of shock and deep, old anger, that frightened her with their intensity. And terrible hurt. Seeing him again brought back the pain she'd lived with for so long, the feeling of being deserted by the first man she'd loved.

"How did you find me?"

"I hired an investigator. He found out your married name, and it wasn't hard, then, to find your address. And the telephone company had a new listing with this address."

"It's a little late, isn't it?" The question that burned in her heart burst out now. "How could you just walk away and forget about me, Oscar?"

She wouldn't call him Dad again. He'd caught her off guard that first moment.

"You have a lot of nerve, turning up at my door like this after years of ignoring the fact that I even existed." She drew a shaky breath so she could say the rest of it. "Why couldn't you have ever sent me a postcard? Why didn't you write to me, or phone or anything?" Old hurt welled up, and her voice trembled. "I was your kid. How could you just walk out and forget I even existed?"

"I did write. Honest to God, I wrote you, Bella. I sent you Christmas presents and birthday gifts, and I even sent an airline ticket once so you could come and visit us. Every single thing came back stamped Return to Sender. I phoned a few times, too, but your mother wouldn't ever let me talk to you. So eventually, I just gave up. I know it was wrong of me, but I couldn't stand getting those letters back all the time."

"You're lying." Bella was shaking so badly she could hardly stand. "I used to wait for the mail, always thinking, hoping there'd be something from you." Tears began to trickle down her cheeks. She brushed them away, ashamed to let him know how much she cared.

"Ahh, Bella. You've got to believe me, I'm telling you the truth." His voice hardened. "Maybe you should talk to your mother. She knows how many times I tried to contact you."

Bella stared at him through a blur of tears. What *was* true here? Could Mae have deliberately cut off contact between her and her father? Could she have been that devious, that cruel?

No. Even Mae wouldn't do that. Bella shook her head. "I don't believe you."

"Look at these, Bella. They're the letters I wrote." He reached inside his coat and brought out a brown envelope secured with a rubber band. He held it out and Bella stared at it. She felt dizzy.

Slowly, she reached out and took the thick bundle. She unsnapped the elastic and pulled out an envelope, with her name nearly obliterated by a blue post-office stamp.

Return to Sender.

There were at least a dozen other envelopes there.

Bella's understanding of what was real and true suddenly disintegrated. Mae had deceived her big-time. Before she could really get her mind around such a monumental betrayal, Josh called down.

"Mom?" He was standing on the stairs, listening. "Mom, are you okay?"

He was being protective. Bella looked up at her son, and in that moment she saw the fine, strong man he would become. Love for him, pride in him, slowed her trembling. She didn't need Oscar now. She had a family of her own.

"Yeah, Josh. I'm fine, thanks." There was

nothing to do except introduce Oscar. "Josh, this is…" She paused. She wanted both of her kids here before she made the introduction. She wanted a moment alone with her father.

"Go up and get Kelsey, would you, please?"

Josh shot a suspicious look at Oscar and raced up the stairs. Bella heard him thump on his sister's bedroom door. "Kelse. Downstairs. Stat."

"I'm warning you," Bella said to Oscar in a low, voice, "don't you dare make any promises to my kids and then break them." They'd been hurt enough.

"I won't." He sounded sincere, but how could she be sure?

In another few moments the teens were there, one on either side of her, and Bella looped her arms protectively around their shoulders, the packet of letters still clutched in one hand. She needed to look at it, read what he'd written. But not right now. All that mattered now was that she believed him. And she did.

She cleared her throat. "Kelsey, Josh, this… umm." She had to swallow the sobs, compose herself enough to say, "This is my father, Oscar Howard. Your…" Her throat constricted, and she gulped. "He's your grandfather."

"The one that walked out on you and Nana?" Josh was still scrutinizing him.

"That would be me, all right." Oscar nodded. "I have a lot of making up to do."

Josh nodded in turn, still holding back, but Kelsey put her hand out and gave Oscar a winning smile.

"Hi," she said shyly, "I'm Kelsey. Can we call you Grandpa?"

"I'd love it. And I'm so happy to meet you." Oscar swiped his hand over the tears trickling down his cheeks. "I can't tell you what this moment means to me." He took Kelsey's hand and tried to draw her closer, but she pulled away. It was too soon for hugs.

He turned to Josh and put a hand on the boy's shoulder.

To Bella's surprise, Josh left it there.

"You're a fine-looking young man, son. You have the look of my own father about you."

"I do?" Josh was taken aback. He'd never known a grandfather, and now, all of a sudden, he was being reminded there'd been a great-grandfather. He recovered fast and asked, a little belligerently, "So where've you been all this time?"

Bella thought it wasn't a bad question, even if it was rude.

"Florida. My wife—my second wife—was sick for a long time. She died two weeks ago."

Bella realized they were all still standing in the entrance hall. "Maybe we should sit down. Can I take your hat and coat…Dad?"

The look he gave her spoke volumes.

Kelsey sat beside Oscar on the sofa, still keeping her distance, but obviously eager to know him.

Oscar addressed his grandchildren. "You're probably wondering why I didn't come back a long time ago to meet you," he began. "Simple truth is, I had no money to travel. See, I was married to a wonderful woman called Dinah. She had a disease for many years, and the medical bills were bad. I worked as a handyman, and when she was able, Dinah took in sewing." He wiped again at his eyes. Kelsey got up and found him a box of tissues.

"Thanks, honey." He blew his nose, a boisterous honk that Bella remembered so well.

Then he went on. "I didn't know that she'd taken out a small insurance policy, so when she died there was money enough to come to Vancouver."

He gave Bella a long look. "Dinah knew I thought about you every single day, and wondered how your life was going." He turned his attention back to Josh and Kelsey. "See, I didn't know Bella was married, or that I had two beautiful grandkids."

Josh said, "Why didn't you just phone and ask Nana?"

"Well…" Oscar hesitated, and then murmured, "Mae and I aren't exactly on speaking terms, I'm afraid."

"Yeah, they're, like, sworn enemies. Nana told

me all about it," Kelsey said with a sigh. "My dad's gone away for a while, too, you know. Like you did."

Kelsey's words were a knife through Bella's heart. The girl never for a moment admitted that Gordon might not come back. But how many years had it taken for Bella herself to admit that Oscar was gone for good? The last thing she'd ever want was for her daughter to suffer the pain she'd felt.

"Your husband… He's not with you?" Oscar looked at Bella, and she shook her head.

Josh said in a bitter tone, "He's gone and left us. I guess it runs in the family. Our dad walked out on us, just the way you did on Nana."

"But our father's coming back," Kelsey insisted, scowling at her brother.

Josh just rolled his eyes. "What planet are your living on?"

Oscar looked sad. "I'm sorry to hear that. About your father."

"We think he's in Mexico," Kelsey volunteered. "We haven't heard from him yet, but we will—right, Mom?"

Bella didn't respond. She ached for her kids, almost more than she could bear.

Josh said to Oscar, "So are *you* gonna stick around now?"

"I am. I sold our trailer before I left, and I have

no reason to go back to Florida. I'm looking around for a place to live."

Kelsey blurted, "We've got lots of spare rooms. You could come and live—"

Josh cut her off. "Shut up, blabbermouth."

"—here," Kelsey finished, glaring at her brother. "Right, Mom?"

"I don't know, Kelsey. We're going to be moving pretty soon, ourselves."

Bella might believe that Oscar wasn't the traitor she'd always thought, but she wasn't quite ready to have him move in, any more than she was ready to have Mae living with her. "It might be better if your grandfather found somewhere on his own."

"I agree. But thank you, anyway, Kelsey." Oscar smiled at her. "It's kind of you. Your mother's right—it's best if I live by myself."

"But you'll come and visit us?"

Her daughter's eagerness brought home to Bella how hungry Kelsey and Josh were for extended family. The only relative they had was Mae. Gordon's parents had died before Bella had met him. During those long, sleepless nights she'd experienced lately, she had wondered how much losing both of them at a relatively early age had affected him.

Oscar said, "I want to spend as much time as I can with you, honey."

Kelsey whined, "So, Mom, why *can't* Grandpa live here?"

"He'll come and see you. He and I need to talk. And you two have homework, so off you go. It's getting late."

Josh bolted for the stairs, but Kelsey went reluctantly.

"Night, Grandpa," she said. With a resentful look directed at Bella, she added, "See you again really soon, okay?"

When Bella and Oscar were alone, she sat and looked at him, wondering where to start. How did you get to know a parent who'd been absent more than half your life? Someone you'd loved and longed for, hated, resented and blamed? And didn't really know at this point.

"I should have taken you with me when I left," he finally said, with a deep sigh. "I knew it at the time, but I also knew your mother would have had me arrested."

Bella snorted. "Get real, Dad. You left with Dinah Flynn, and I don't think she'd have been overjoyed to drag a teenager along."

"Dinah wouldn't have minded one bit." Oscar leaned forward, elbows on his knees in a posture Bella remembered. "I really wish you'd have been able to know her, Bella. She was a very special lady."

"Mom always said she was…" Bella stopped

abruptly. What Mae had said about Dinah wasn't something she should repeat to Oscar, who'd obviously loved the woman.

And now Bella had to wonder if anything her mom had told her was true. She grew dizzy, trying to figure out the depths of deception Mae had stooped to.

"Your mother never remarried?"

"Nope. She never got over you leaving. You hurt her pretty bad." That, at least, was true. Bella had never realized how deep the hurt must have been until the same thing happened to her.

"Your mother and I didn't have a good marriage, Bella. It was as much my fault as hers. Leaving as I did was wrong, just walking out without any warning, but at the time I couldn't see any other way."

"Yeah, well, you left her, but you *deserted* me. I was your kid and I loved you. How could you do that?" Bella wasn't about to let him off the hook. "And you must have known that finances were going to be a problem. You must have known we'd be short of money."

The more things change, the more they stay the same. According to Mae.

"What was the problem between you two?"

"Oh, lots of different things. For one, your mother was a bit of a spendthrift."

So Mae wasn't the only one laying blame. Bella

bristled and defended her. "That's not true. After you left, Mom did her best. She had a really hard time supporting us, and she did without lots of stuff so I could have things."

"I didn't have much, Bella, but I did try and send your mother support money for you. She sent it back, along with everything else. Didn't even bother to see what was in the envelopes. It was just returned unopened, straight from the post office."

Bella shook her head. "But she had no right to do that."

"No, she didn't. But there wasn't much I could do about it." Oscar sighed. "I finally hired a lawyer, but I had to let him go, since it was costing more than I could afford and there didn't seem to be much he could do. If I'd been here in Vancouver, it might have been different, but I was in Florida."

Money again. Bella knew a lot about what a person could and couldn't afford. She'd learned that lesson really well since Gordon left.

"So what I did instead was put a little money away for you off each paycheck," Oscar was saying. "It was Dinah's idea. She said it was better than wasting it on lawyer's fees." He pulled out his wallet from his back pocket and removed a check, which he handed to Bella. "It's not much, I'm afraid."

Stunned, she stared at it—$5,804.32. Her first

thought was that she could pay Mae back. Bella really didn't want to owe her anything, particularly after finding out how dishonest her mother had been. But…

"I can't take this." She tried to hand it back to him.

He folded his hands and shook his head. "Please, Bella. It means a lot to me. It can't make up for the years I was gone, when I should have been getting to know you, supporting you. But at least it's something."

She could see by his yearning expression how much he wanted her to accept it. She hesitated. And then she folded it in half and tucked it in her pants pocket. "Thank you, Dad."

"You are so welcome, *Bella mia*." The warm, crooked smile she remembered flashed across his face. "Now, how about telling me what I missed in your life? What was your high-school graduation like? Did you go to college?"

"I'll get us some coffee first. Decaf okay?"

"Decaf is perfect. Let me help you."

He followed her to the kitchen, and they loaded a tray with mugs and some of Kelsey's chocolate chip cookies. Bella remembered times when she was a child, sneaking around the kitchen making hot chocolate with him after Mae had gone to bed. He'd always smelled strongly of Old Spice, and he still did. She'd thought that was the way all daddies smelled.

By the time the coffee was ready, Bella felt she had begun to know him again. She remembered the way he moved with a peculiar grace, the way he tilted his head to one side, listening intently to what she said, the single decisive nod when he agreed with her.

They sat in the living room, and she began to tell him about some of the high points of her life. She'd gotten as far as art school when the phone rang.

It was Mae, and every muscle in Bella's body tensed. Her mother had some explaining to do, but now was not the time. All the same, it was really hard to speak to her calmly.

"I hope you've come to your senses about selling that house yourself, Annabella," she began. "Why not let that nice young man who's helping with the repairs list it for you? Or there's always Beatrice's son—he's in real estate and he's trustworthy. It's foolhardy to try and do it yourself. You have no idea—"

Bella interrupted, trying to keep her voice steady. "Sorry, but someone's here just now. I'll have to call you back later."

"Not too much later. You know I go to bed at ten. Is it someone about the house?"

"I'll call you. This is not a good time."

Bella hung up before Mae had a chance to say anything else.

"That was Mom," she said, simply. How odd to talk to her mother on the phone with her father sitting right in the room. If Mae knew, she'd erupt like a volcano. And Bella still had some volcanic feelings of her own.

He nodded. "I suppose Mae's still mad at me."

"Yeah, I'd say so." Mad was an understatement. Hate was more like it, and even that was putting it mildly, when Mae took to ranting about him.

"We weren't a good match. All we did was squabble. Now with Dinah, we hardly had a harsh word, all these years."

Bella still felt a sense of betrayal each time he said the other woman's name. How could she be protective of Mae, and furious with her at the same time?

"Why did you leave without even saying good-bye to me?" She thought she'd gotten beyond the hurt that had caused, but when she asked her father this question, the pain was as intense as it had been all those years ago. "I came home from school that day, and you were gone. I guess I always thought it was my fault, somehow."

"Your fault? Oh, honey, how could it be your fault? I was just too much of a coward to face you, was all." He rubbed a hand through his hair. "I knew you'd cry, and then I wasn't sure I could go through with it. And I felt as if I was dying, living with Mae. But leaving you was the hardest thing

I've ever done. Damn, I made such a mess of things. I'm so sorry." He got up and tentatively pulled her to her feet. Then he put his arms around her, and she realized how much she wanted that.

"I'm sorry, too." He held her until she pulled away. He sat down again. "Do you have any pictures of Kelsey and Josh from when they were younger?"

"Tons." Bella got some albums from the hall cupboard. She started with the hospital photos, and she'd reached nursery school when the phone rang again.

"Bella?" Charlie had an excellent telephone voice, and warmth spread through her. "I just wanted to tell you again that I really enjoyed our dinner, in spite of my daughter and her attitude problem."

"I enjoyed it, too."

His tone was relaxed, intimate. Lonely? "So are you just sitting around watching the idiot box, same as me?"

"No, no. I…I have company."

"Hey, sorry to bother you."

"It's my father," she said quickly, knowing Charlie was about to hang up.

"Your *father*?" He sounded as surprised as she still felt. "Where'd he spring from? Do you need me to come over?"

"No." But the fact that he'd offered, reassured

her. "No, he just got into town. From Florida. We're looking at baby pictures. Of my kids."

"I'll let you get back at it, then. But if you need anything, just call. Even to talk. Anytime. I'm a light sleeper."

Bella felt comforted. And aroused. But how could she feel aroused with her father sitting right there? Damn Charlie, with his husky voice and his "call anytime."

She went back to the snapshots, and it was after eleven when Oscar finally called a cab to take him back to his hotel.

Bella felt guilty and sad, watching him as he hurried down the winding sidewalk to the curb, where the yellow taxi was waiting. He was huddled into a coat that was far too flimsy for a cold, damp Vancouver night, and he looked old and thin. And terribly alone.

There were empty bedrooms upstairs. She could have asked him to stay. She *should* have asked him to stay.

But then again, all the excuses in the world didn't make up for all those years of silence. Some small part of her felt that he could have tried harder.

And then there was Mae. It was difficult for Bella to get her mind around the fact that her mother had lied to her for years—and was still lying. She had denied Bella the right to make her own decisions about Oscar. Mae had sent mail back when it wasn't hers to refuse; she'd denied her grandchildren a relationship with their grandfather. The extent of her mother's treachery was mind-boggling. What a pair to have as parents.

Bella poured herself another cup of coffee and sat down at the island in the kitchen. She opened the top envelope from the stack Oscar had given her, and tears came to her eyes. It was a birthday card with red roses on it. "Happy Sixteenth" was emblazoned across the front in gold.

"My dearest Bella mia," the enclosed note began. Tears came to Bella's eyes.

I hope you get this, honey. Your birthday is coming in another week and I think of you every day. I can hardly believe you're sixteen. It seems yesterday I held you in the hospital, so small and beautiful. I miss you very much and I hope someday you find it in your heart to forgive me for leaving the way I did. I hope that your mother doesn't send this back the way she has the other mail.

I love you. Happy birthday.

Your loving father, Oscar. Please call me collect anytime….

Bella opened another letter, and another, and with each one her heart broke all over again, for the lonely, confused girl who'd wrongly believed her father had abandoned her. And her anger at Mae expanded until it felt like a balloon that was ready to burst inside her.

In each letter, Oscar reiterated how much he loved her. In one of the first, he told her he and Dinah had rented a two-bedroom trailer so Bella could come and visit. And as each successive letter was returned, as his phone calls to her were refused, his frustration with Mae became more evident.

Bella laid the last one down and stared at the stack of letters. She wanted to phone Mae right that moment and confront her with the evidence. But a glance at the clock showed that it was twenty after twelve. Dragging her mother out of bed at this hour wouldn't make a lot of sense—Mae took a sleeping pill every night, and she'd be groggy and incoherent.

Bella wanted her wide-awake and aware when they had this particular conversation. And she wasn't going to do it on the phone, she decided. She wanted to see Mae's face when the entire truth was revealed. What possible excuse could she have for her actions?

But Bella needed to talk to *someone* about this. Niki and Tom were in Victoria for the week, going through another round of fertility tests.

Which left Charlie. Maybe she'd known all along she was going to call him. She resisted one more minute, just to prove to herself she could, and then dialed.

CHAPTER NINE

"HI, BELLA." At least Charlie sounded wide-awake.

"How'd you know it was me?"

"I have caller ID."

For a moment, she couldn't think what to say, where or how to begin. She got up and walked into the living room.

Fortunately, Charlie helped her out. "Your father still there?"

"No. He's staying at a hotel. My God, it was such a shock to see him. He just walked up to the door."

"I can imagine. How long has it been?"

She sat down in the armchair. "Almost twenty years without a word. I barely even thought about him anymore." As soon as she said it, she knew it was a lie. She'd thought about him more than ever, especially since Gordon left. Funny how one abandonment made you think of the other.

"Did he say why he never contacted you?"

"He says he tried to phone me, sent me letters,

even a plane ticket once, but my mother sent everything back. She must have somehow had a different address for anything that came from him, because I used to watch the mail that came to the house. Is that possible, do you think?"

"Sure. The post office does it in cases where a partner doesn't want contact with a previous spouse. They establish a mailing address, and whatever comes from the person is rerouted to that box and automatically sent back to sender."

"That's what she must have done." Fresh hurt washed through Bella, and she leaned forward and hugged her knees. "It's such a mean thing to do—to him, and especially to me. She knew how much I loved him, how I waited for something from him. She must have known how I slowly lost all hope."

"Well, he cared about you, and it was a way to hurt him. The way she was probably hurt."

Bella thought about that, and admitted to herself it could be true. A little of her rage at Mae disappeared. "You sound like a shrink."

"Drugstore variety. It rubs off. I saw one for a while after the accident, and you pick up on the things they say, which is mostly, 'how does that make you feel?' But I was drinking, so it didn't do me much good. I learned the lingo, though."

Bella closed her eyes. "Hurt or not, I'm still mad at Mae, Charlie. I'm just so bloody mad at her."

"Yeah. Well, you've got reason to be. What are you going to do?"

"Confront her. Let her know I know, and tell her exactly how I feel. Possibly break something heavy over her old, stubborn head."

"And what about your father? How do you feel about him?"

Bella paused. "I don't know yet. I guess I'm still mad at him, too. Whatever excuses he makes, he did just give up on me after a while. I guess he almost seems too good to be true. Apparently his second wife was sick, and that took up a lot of time and money."

"What did she have?"

"Multiple sclerosis."

"I guess, without insurance, it can be pretty expensive to be sick in the U.S."

Why did he have to defuse all her anger? "They could have come back here. He didn't say why they didn't. He gave me some money he'd saved for me, though. It...it means a lot— not just the money, but the idea that he'd do that. Put it away for me. Even though he didn't have that much."

"Sounds like he thought about you a lot, even if he wasn't in touch."

"Yeah." She sighed. "But I still think he could have found me sooner. Don't you, Charlie? I mean, if you left the country, wouldn't you search for Emma till you found her? Would you just give up the way he did?"

There was silence for a long moment. "Tough question. Circumstances are different for everyone. Did I ever tell you that after Alice and I split, Emma didn't speak to me for a year and a half? That was the hardest time of my life. At first I tried really hard to contact her, but after a while I just wore down. Sometimes you have to let time do the work. With a sick wife, I'd guess that things weren't too easy for your dad, either. What kind of work does he do? I guess he'd be retired by now?"

She didn't know. She hadn't asked. She realized she'd been pretty self-centered about things, and suddenly felt a stab of regret. "When I was a kid, he worked in construction. In Florida, he was some kind of handyman, he said. So no pension, I guess."

"Maybe he'd be interested in helping us out with the properties. We could pay him for the work, when they sell."

"Maybe." Bella wasn't sure how she felt about that. She wasn't sure how much contact she really wanted with Oscar. "And maybe we'll all go totally bankrupt and end up in debtors' prison."

Charlie laughed. He had a great laugh, and it made her smile a little.

"No way. I'm confident that with your brains

and my strong back, we're going to do really well with those loser houses, Bella. And besides, there is no debtors' prison anymore."

"What a relief."

He laughed again. It felt comfortable and comforting, talking to him. And arousing. Why did he always make her aware of her sexuality?

"I didn't wake you up, did I?" It was a little late to ask.

"Nope. I was sitting here reading."

She leaned back, imagining him slouched in a chair. "Reading what?"

"Murder mystery. Ruth Rendall. I like the forensic stuff, now that I don't have to be involved in any of it."

"You ever think about going back? Into police work?"

"Never. I might not be an ace at selling real estate, but it's got police work beat all to hell, in my opinion. As a cop, all you see is the negative stuff, and before long you start to view everything and everyone suspiciously. It kind of gets to your soul."

"Like money problems. They've sure shriveled mine."

"Well, if it's any consolation, my mom has a saying—that you never see a U-Haul being towed behind a hearse."

Bella laughed. "That's one Mae doesn't know.

I'll have to tell it to her. After I smack her upside
the head." She'd have bet anything, when she'd
made this call, that nothing could have made her
laugh tonight or feel kinder toward her mother, but
he'd managed it.

Bella thought of something else she'd wondered about. "Does your mother still live here in
Vancouver?"

"Lucille? Not really. She spends time here now
and then, but she doesn't actually live anywhere.
She'll stay with Rick or me when she's in town,
but never for more than a couple weeks. She has
a few boxes of stuff stored in Rick's basement. She
does house-sitting and sometimes works as a
short-order cook, but mostly she travels." There
was such warmth and fondness in his voice. It was
obvious he held no grudges whatsoever toward
his mother.

So, maybe Bella was going to have to get over
hers. Mae was, after all, the only mom she would
ever have. And she had her good points, although
at the moment it was tough to recall any of them.

"What an exciting way to spend your retire-
ment." But Bella wondered how Lucille could
afford to travel. Hadn't Charlie once told her his
mother had supported them by working as a wait-
ress?

He said, "It isn't my idea of a good time, but it
suits her, and that's all that matters. Mom's pretty

unusual. She does exactly what she wants to do, and manages on very little money. She lives on her government pensions. She's an expert on Greyhound bus routes, she's a member of Elderhostel and she works as an airline courier, taking documents to different places. Her return airfare is paid, and she gets to visit different parts of the world. Rick and Sharon are horrified by the way she lives, and they keep offering her money or asking her to move in with them, but Mom loves her independence."

"Lucky her. Lucky you. I wish Mae were more like that. If I'd so much as let my guard down for an instant, she'd move in here. And now I get the feeling Oscar would, too. Yikes."

Charlie chuckled. "It'd be interesting, having them both living with you, no?"

"No!" Bella let out a small shriek at the thought. "Not in this lifetime. Besides, I'll probably end up in a tent in Pigeon Park myself, after this house sells. I doubt they'd like that much."

"Calm down, we'll make sure it's a really nice tent. They have some with separate rooms now."

"Thanks so much." She felt almost optimistic, instead of furious. "On that note, I better go to bed. And let you do the same."

"Yeah. See you tomorrow, probably. I'll buy you lunch—gotta keep your strength up. Painting's hard work."

Bella hung up, still smiling. He was such a nice man. But as Niki once said, they were all Prince Charming until you started living with them and found out they dropped wet towels and dirty underwear on the floor.

Living with Charlie wasn't going to happen, anyway, so she could just go on enjoying him, no strings. Right?

NO STRINGS, Charlie reminded himself as he hung up the phone. He had to keep it that way, regardless of how much she appealed to him. His life was complicated enough, without taking on a whole new family. And he still needed to find a way to discourage her from selling that house herself.

His attraction to her was a strange phenomenon, because Bella was a prickly, intense and complicated woman. He'd always assumed that easygoing, free-flowing, slightly independent women would be more his type—Alice's exact opposite.

Bella was way beyond slightly independent. He practically had to arm wrestle her to get her to let him help with anything. Funny how eager he was to help Bella, and how reluctant when it came to Alice.

His ex-wife was off the charts when it came to needy. Charlie felt sorry for her, but he was getting increasingly tired of the emotional blackmail she was so good at doling out. Trouble was, he'd established a pattern there, and patterns were tough to break.

Bella, on the other hand, intrigued him, even with her fierce independence, bad temper and all. He found her sexy as hell. He very much wanted to take her to bed, although a viable method had so far eluded him. Her house came with teenagers, and his... Well, his place wasn't such a good idea, either.

Emma had an unnerving habit of turning up at his door unexpectedly. He'd have to do something about that, too, but like Alice and her demands, he hadn't decided exactly how to go about it yet.

Yawning, he set aside his book, turned off the lights and made his way to the bedroom. The rented apartment was small, in one of the older buildings on Main Street. On the positive side, it was cheap and had come furnished. On the debit side, it was noisy and dingy.

Not exactly a romantic hideaway. But if worst came to worst—or best came to best—he'd bring Bella here. At least the bed didn't squeak.

He began imagining trying to make it squeak, and was almost asleep when the phone rang again.

"Daddy?" Emma's panicky voice brought him upright, feet on the floor, heart hammering with dread. She hadn't called him Daddy since her early teens.

"Daddy, I'm at the General. Mom's taken pills. Please, can you come?"

CHAPTER TEN

ALICE HAD SWALLOWED a cocktail of Nembutal, Effexor, sleeping pills and Valium. In Emergency, she'd had her stomach pumped and they'd put her on a drip, and by the time Charlie arrived, she was far too exhausted to speak to anyone.

Emma, on the other hand, did nothing but talk.

"Where were you? I tried your cell, and as usual, you weren't picking up. And your home phone was busy for hours!" Her voice rose. "I kept trying the cell—how come you didn't answer?"

There were half a dozen other people in the waiting room, and to their credit, none turned to stare. Instead, they averted their eyes.

"I was home," Charlie said quietly. "I must have left the cell phone in the truck. I'd been home for quite a while."

"On the phone to that woman friend of yours, I suppose." Emma made the words *woman friend* sound like "cheap slut."

A young doctor appeared beside them before Charlie had time to respond.

"Ms. Fredricks?"

Emma nodded. "This is my father, Charlie Fredricks." And her hand wormed its way into his.

Charlie gave it a reassuring squeeze.

"I'm Dr. Sui—I'm the psych resident. Call me Claire, why don't you? I wonder if I could have a word with you both?" She led the way to a closet-size examining room, ushered them inside and shut the door.

"Mrs. Fredricks is out of physical danger and her condition is stable. Her electrolytes are still out of whack, but that's not life-threatening. A social worker has seen her, but she isn't able to talk much just yet. In all cases of attempted suicide, we transfer the patient to the psych ward, and we're going to take her up there now. I wanted to ask if either of you know what might have precipitated tonight's attempt?"

Emma waited, and when Charlie didn't say anything, she said in a strained voice, "My mom's been unhappy for a long time. I...I'm a student at UBC, and I was supposed to go over after classes tonight and have dinner, but I had too much homework and an exam in the morning." Her voice quavered. "So I called her and asked if we could do it tomorrow, instead. She said sure, and she didn't sound any different than usual. Pretty down, but she often is. But then later she called me, and she was…she was incoherent. She dropped the phone, and I couldn't hang up. So I borrowed my friend's cell phone and called 911. And then I tried to call my father, but he wasn't…" She shot an accusatory look at Charlie. "He wasn't available. By the time I got to her place, the ambulance had already brought her here. It was my fault. I should have gone over there."

Charlie put an arm around Emma's shoulders and squeezed. "I'm sorry, honey. I'm sorry I didn't get the call."

She crumpled suddenly, leaning against him, and he could feel shudders, all the way down her spine.

Charlie's heart ached. How had they come to this, he and Alice? Emma was their daughter, and surely a child shouldn't be responsible for her parents' well-being. A surge of anger at Alice made him recoil, and then he felt guilty for not being more compassionate. She had been desperate enough to try and take her own life—surely he could sympathize?

Dr. Sui turned to Charlie. "Did you notice anything unusual about your wife today?"

He shook his head. "I didn't see her today. Alice and I are divorced. We have been for three years now. We live separately, although I usually see her almost daily. I spoke to her earlier today—she wanted a storm door put on the basement. She didn't sound any different than usual." But "usual" with Alice was never cheerful, so how could he judge her mood? "I was busy, so I didn't go over."

The way she wanted. The way she always wants.

"I see. And neither of you can think of a precipitating factor that might have made Alice choose today to decide to swallow pills?"

Charlie shook his head.

"She didn't mention that anything unusual had happened," Emma said. She sounded bone weary. "But she's been depressed for quite a while now."

"Okay, thank you both. Why don't you go home, get some rest? As I said, your mother will be taken up to psych, Emma, and you'll be able to visit her tomorrow. We'll take good care of her. Is there anyone else she's close to—her mother…a sister?"

Emma said, "Gram and Grampa live in Chilliwack, and I didn't want to scare them this late at night—they're not so young anymore. Auntie Lorraine is on Vancouver Island, but she and Mom aren't close. And Uncle John—well, he doesn't have much to do with Mom, either. They barely speak." Her voice wobbled. "She really only has me."

Charlie knew exactly why Alice's friends and family had distanced themselves. Her constant neediness had worn everyone thin.

When they were outside the hospital, he suggested Emma come and spend the night with him.

"I can't. I have this major exam in sociology at ten tomorrow, and it determines sixty percent of our mark. I have to take it and I need to get back to the residence."

"Okay, I'll drive you over, and then I'll bring your car to you first thing tomorrow." She had an old, but reliable Honda Civic he'd bought her the year before. "Give me the keys and tell me where it's parked."

"Okay." She pointed out the lot and handed over the keys before they climbed into Charlie's truck. Nothing more was said until they were well away from the hospital.

Emma heaved a huge sigh. "Do you think she'll try again, Dad?"

"Absolutely not." He shook his head, although he wasn't at all sure. "I think this is probably the best thing that could happen, in the long run. I've suggested lots of times that your mom go talk to someone, but she always refused. I think now she'll be forced to get the help she needs."

Emma said in a belligerent tone, "You make her sound pathetic. She wasn't the one who walked out on the marriage, you know. You did. She's lonely. You're not drinking now, and maybe if you'd move back home you could both get counseling and make it work. But you won't even try."

"Emma." Charlie had had more than enough. "Your mother and I are divorced, and that's final. There won't be any reconciliation. I help her all I can, I support her generously, and I'll do whatever is necessary to make certain she gets the help she needs, but I am *not* moving back. And I'm tired of your attitude. Whatever is troubling your mother now is not my fault." At least he'd gotten that far in his own counseling sessions. "It's her stuff, and she's going to have to deal with it."

"So are you going to marry that person you were with at the restaurant?"

It took a lot of self-control to hold his temper. "Her name is Bella Monroe and we're business partners, nothing more." Not yet.

He explained about the run-down houses. "As far as marriage goes, it's not something I plan on doing again, with Bella or with anyone. I'm not good at it. I admit I was a lousy husband to your mother." He waited a beat, and then added, "But the marriage wasn't working—your mother and I just weren't compatible. Policemen let their jobs consume them, and I was no exception. The more I worked, the needier your mother became. I tried to encourage her to get a job, get out more, but she refused."

"She liked being at home with me."

"I know, sweetheart." He didn't have the heart to remind Emma that she'd been in school since she was five, and many years had passed since staying at home for their daughter's sake made any sense.

Instead, Charlie said gently, "I'm single, Emma, and I'm entitled to have friends, male and female. And I shouldn't have to tell you that I'd like you to treat them with respect."

He stopped at a light and glanced over at Emma. Shiny tear tracks marked her cheeks, and she swiped a hand across her eyes and sniffled.

"There's tissues in the glove box," he said.

"I just feel so sorry for Mom," she wailed, digging for the tissues and crying harder than ever. "I always feel I ought to be there more, keep her company, you know? If I'd gone over tonight, the way I promised, none of this would have happened."

He hadn't realized just how much she felt responsible. He hadn't admitted to himself the extent of Alice's dependence on their daughter.

Charlie pulled the truck over to the curb and gathered her into his arms.

"Emma, I know this sounds harsh, but you're not responsible for your mother, for her happiness or her well-being. Or for mine, either. You're only responsible for yourself, sweetheart."

"Is that what they tell you at those AA meetings?" Her tone was still challenging, but she was settled in his arms, her head on his chest.

"Yeah. That and other good mind-bending

junk." He didn't go to many meetings these days, but the philosophy stuck with him because it made sense. It worked. It didn't take away the guilt he felt for his part in what had become of Alice, but that was his own burden to bear.

"Your mom's going to be okay. I know her, and I know how strong she can be." He knew, too, how controlling and manipulative Alice was, and he was deeply angry at her for what she was doing to Emma, but he didn't say so.

"Your mom is perfectly safe, and she'll get the help she needs. Start thinking of yourself—of what *you* need, honey."

After a while he let her go, and pulled into traffic again. The clock on the dash read 3:16. "There's not much left of the night, but you should go to bed and get some sleep, and then ace that exam in the morning, okay?"

Emma sighed, a deep, hopeless sound. "I'll try, Dad."

"That's my girl." He pulled up in front of her dorm and walked her to the entrance. It was starting to rain.

"Night, Daddy." Her goodbye brought tears to his eyes.

"See you tomorrow." He tried to give her a hug, but she pulled away.

The door locked behind her, and she waved at him through the glass.

He watched until she got in the elevator. Not only was he a total screwup when it came to marriage, Charlie thought miserably as he loped back to the truck. He was also a world-class loser at parenting. And unless he managed to sell something fairly soon, he was going to have to admit defeat at the real-estate thing. Right or wrong, he had his hopes pinned on Bella in that department.

For the rest of it, he'd have to find a way to help his daughter. He couldn't change the past, but he could damn well work hard on the present.

"OH. MY. STARS."

It was Wednesday. Monroe's Hardware was no more, and Charlie had taken Bella for lunch at a neighborhood café before driving here to the first east side property he wanted her to see.

Wanted her to resurrect.

From the outside, the gray stucco single-story house looked similar to the others in the working-class neighborhood. But once the battered front door squeaked open and Bella stepped inside, the full extent of the disaster was apparent. They were in the living room, and Charlie watched as she took in her surroundings.

"Who in their right mind would paint a ceiling purple? And walls orange? And that green carpet—what's underneath that? Because it's got to go. It looks like someone was murdered in here. *What* are those stains?"

Charlie had seen the place before, but even so, it was unnerving to view it again. He pulled out a notebook and started a list. *Rip out rug.*

"Far as I know, it's not blood. It looks like oil-based paint to me. The last renter fancied himself an artist, maybe?"

"Try color-blind druggie," Bella corrected. "And why would he tear off these steps?" She'd opened the sliding door, which was a major feature of one wall of the living room, only to discover a sheer three-foot drop to the wall-to-wall concrete that constituted the side garden.

"Security?" Charlie had wondered that himself. "Didn't want his paintings stolen?"

Rebuild steps, he scribbled in his notebook.

Bella gave him a pained look and went down the hallway, peering into the bathroom. "What's the purpose of that hole in the wall?"

She bent over to peer out at the view the small gap afforded of the neighbor's fence, and Charlie appreciated the way her jeans clung to her. There wasn't all that much there, but what was there was certainly shapely.

Fix hole in bathroom wall.

"Ventilation? Couldn't afford air freshener?" Charlie looked out, as well, down to a pile of plastic bags on the ground. "Garbage disposal?"

"Dump." She wrinkled her nose. "And it smells like something's going rotten. You did check for bodies, right?"

Check for bodies. Get rid of garbage.

"Rotting floorboards," Charlie guessed. "The taps were left on and water ruined the floor. Lucky it was uneven, because it must have poured into the basement instead of flooding the entire main floor. Which has probably caused a major mold problem downstairs."

"What happened to the trim around the doors?"

"By the size of the teeth marks, I'd say the guy who lived here had a bull mastiff that liked the taste of molding."

Replace molding.

Bella was now in the kitchen, staring at the Pepto-Bismol pink walls and the backsplash behind the sink. "I didn't know tile came in that shade of turquoise."

"Maybe going for a retro look?"

"Maybe going for a wrecking crew. This place is truly awful, Charlie."

"So, the question is, can we fix it? Remember, fast and cheap are the key words."

She shrugged. "Patch it. Paint it. Clean it. Do something with the cement outside. How do people live like this?"

"You got me. How long do you figure it'll take us?"

"The rest of our lives?" She flung her hands in the air, palms up. "God, Charlie, I don't know. Two weeks, working full-time, day and night?"

"I love your optimism. Did you ask your father if he's interested in helping?"

Her expression changed, becoming guarded. "I haven't seen him again. I called his hotel, but he wasn't there. He'd checked out."

"Weird. Are you worried?"

"About Oscar?" She blew a raspberry, but Charlie could tell it was a cover up. She didn't meet his eyes. "Why would I worry about him disappearing for three days when he's already been gone for so long?"

And why would he notice Alice was depressed when she'd been that way for most of their marriage?

"Your mother know yet that he's back?"

Bella shook her head. "Not unless he told her himself. And if he did, that could very well be why he's missing. I've been too busy the past couple of days to talk to anyone. Getting the store cleared out and shut down was major. And then I thought it would be smart to wait before I talked to Mae. Until I felt a little less like hitting her with an ax."

"Wise decision. How are the kids doing?"

"Up and down. They're both asking where Grandpa is, damn his hide. He appears, meets them and then disappears, it's one more big disappointment for them. Josh isn't skipping school that I know of—so far so good. Kelsey gives me plenty of attitude, but she also cooked dinner for me two nights in a row."

"Daughters are something, aren't they?" Charlie was thinking of Emma. He'd gone to the psych ward each evening since Alice had been admitted, and Emma was always there. She'd looked tired and sad. Older than her years.

He'd had a private meeting with the psychologist. He'd told Dr. Sui he was worried sick, not about Alice but about Emma. He'd blurted out that the girl had no life of her own; she felt responsible for her mother so much that he was afraid her personal life and even her education were being affected.

"I understand your concerns, and they're absolutely valid, but those are issues Emma is going to have to confront on her own, Charlie," the doctor had said. "All I can suggest is counseling—and I have. I feel that Emma would benefit from some group sessions both with and without her mother. Would you be willing to attend, as well, should she want you there?"

"Of course. Absolutely. Anything that would help."

"There's also the matter of your and Alice's codependence. That's something you might want to address."

"How do you mean?"

"It would be good for Alice and for you to examine the ways in which you interact. It's a pattern, and Emma is using it in her own relationships."

"You mean Emma is doing to me what she's seen Alice do?"

"What do you think, Charlie?"

He hadn't thought about it in those terms. He'd blamed his ex-wife for all of it, without considering his own role.

He'd left the psychologist's office feeling more frustrated than ever—but also realizing he needed to reevaluate the way he and Alice managed things.

"Charlie?" Bella's voice interrupted his thoughts. "What about the leak in the corner of the living room? Will you have to replace the roof?"

"Nope, I can probably fix it. I'll climb up and have a look." He changed the subject. "Think Josh would like to come with me one night this week for a game of squash? He said he liked the game."

Charlie couldn't fix things for his daughter, and it hurt. But maybe he could help Josh out a little.

Bella gave him a puzzled look. "You'd have to ask him, but I bet he'd like that."

"Great. Will he be home later tonight?"

"He had basketball right after school, but after that he's home. We all are. I forgot to tell you, some guy's coming over to see the house," Bella added. "With his wife. I'm trying not to get my hopes up."

Damn. That might just screw up Charlie's chances at the listing. But what could he say? "Let me know if he makes you an offer, Bella. If you want, I'll look it over, see if it's fair."

"Thanks." She waved a hand at the basement door. "I need to have a look down there, but if any weird music starts, I'm out of here."

"Good thinking." He switched on the basement light and opened the door. "But let me go first so I can protect you. I brought garlic."

She grinned at him. "I noticed. From that sauce you had on the steak sandwich at lunch, no doubt."

He grimaced. "You really know how to hurt a guy. So much for getting you in one of the upstairs bedrooms and jumping your bones." Oops, he hadn't meant to say that. Thinking it was one thing, blurting it out another.

She kept it light. "In this pigsty? Your idea of a romantic setting leaves a little to be desired."

"I can always dream." He led the way down the stairs and switched on a lightbulb that was hanging from the ceiling.

She followed him and looked around at the partially finished area. Water damage had warped the drywall, mold was visible, the subflooring was rotten and the smell was atrocious.

"This is just disgusting. But at least it matches the rest of the house." She turned toward him. "So is that what you really want, Charlie? To jump my bones?"

Damn. Busted. Warning bells went off in his head. He knew he shouldn't have made that crack. Even in the dim light, he could see that she'd turned red. But she held his gaze and stood her ground.

"See, I just want to know where I stand," Bella stated. "Once in a while you kiss me as if…as if it might go somewhere, but I don't know whether you're serious or that's just the way guys show friendship these days. I'm *so* out of the loop. I mean, I've watched *Sex and the City,* but it seems pretty far-fetched, the clothes and the shoes and the racy conversation. Niki talks like that, but she'd never dream of actually doing anything. She's loved Tom since high school." Bella ran out of breath and rolled her eyes heavenward. "Oh, God, I can't believe I'm saying this to you."

"Are you asking me what my intentions are?" It might have been funny, but he didn't find it that way at all. He was impressed by her bravery—it took a hell of a lot of chutzpah to come right out with something like this. And what was he going to say to her?

"Yeah, I guess I am. Asking." She was looking down at the filth on the floor now, scuffing one sneaker back and forth. "So? You want to sleep with me? Or…or not?"

He tried to figure out what to say that was both honest and diplomatic, and then gave up on it. The truth was the only solution. At least about this.

"I want to take you to bed, Bella," he said softly. "I want that something awful. You're sexy and funny, and I want to find out what turns you on." He drew a shuddering breath. "I want to explore wicked things with you. Naked. In a warm room with a lock on the door." Just talking about it turned *him* on.

He stepped away from her and pretended to explore the rest of the basement, opening doors to musty cubbyholes once intended as bedrooms or workshops. Or torture chambers. It was hard to tell.

He turned back to her. She was staring at him with her eyebrows raised to her hairline.

"Wow. You talk a great fight."

"I'm a lover, not a fighter. At least, I'd like to be. With you." He took a breath and went on in a rough, low tone. "I want to do other things, too, after we've spent a couple eons making love. Like find out what music you enjoy, what books you read, what TV programs you watch." He did want that. "What you were like as a little girl. What you dream about." He moved closer to her and added the rest of what had to be said. "But it's not a good idea. See, as far as forever goes, Bella, I'm just not the right sort of guy. I'm not good at it. One marriage complicated my life, and still does. I'm not about to go there again. So it's probably better if we forget the sex stuff and just stay friends. Business partners."

"Right." She gave one sharp nod. "So this is a decision you get to make all by yourself, is that it? I notice you don't ask me what I'd like. Maybe I just want a short, hot, steamy affair. Did that ever cross your mind? I wasn't exactly asking you to marry me, or were you listening?"

"I was. I just want to be really clear on this. I don't want to start anything with you that might lead to a misunderstanding."

"Misunderstanding, huh?" Her voice was still quiet, but he could feel a storm coming on. "*So*," she said. "You want me to sign an agreement? A presex thing? Like a prenup, but no money involved, right? Promising I'll never bring up the *M* word? Never ask you to spend the night?" Her voice rose. "What do you think I was planning, Charlie? Having unprotected sex, getting pregnant and holding a gun to your head until we found a preacher?"

She must have remembered what he'd told her about him and Alice getting pregnant and then getting married, because she added, "Sorry. Sorry. I didn't mean that part. But you really are arrogant, you know that? Don't you think I've had enough of marriage myself to last me a lifetime? Why would I believe in forever, or even want it with you? Besides, I'm still married. You could get named as correspondent in a divorce! You ought to think about that instead of worrying about getting trapped in another marriage. You...you dumb *man*."

She didn't wait for an answer, but went storming up the steps. And before he could follow, he heard the front door of the house slam.

Hard.

CHAPTER ELEVEN

"Bella, wait."

He took the steps two at a time and was out the front door before he remembered they'd driven here in her car, since he'd dropped his truck off that morning to have the wheels balanced.

"Bella." Shoot. He caught a glimpse of her old red Pontiac fishtailing around the corner.

Damn. Well, the lady had a temper, he knew that. It was almost refreshing, because at least you always knew where you stood. Alice had never shown anger; she'd just gotten silent and sullen, not talking, shooting him accusing glances and staying quiet for weeks. He'd gone nuts trying to guess what was wrong between them—and the answer, he knew now, was being married to each other. Or being married at all. So he was gun-shy and he had good reason.

But he was damned if he could figure out what exactly he'd said to Bella that was so inflammatory. If he lived to a hundred and fifteen, he'd never understand women.

He hauled out his cell phone, which he was now keeping on and in his jacket pocket, and called Yellow Cab.

BELLA GOT TO THE SECOND intersection before she cooled off enough to really think over what Charlie had said. The first part, all that stuff about her being desirable, had made her assume he was talking about somebody else. The second part… Well, somehow she'd thought he was trying to let her down easy, and all she'd really heard was the stuff about not getting married and not wanting a sexual relationship with her.

But when she went back over it, hadn't he actually been saying he *wanted* to make love to her? With no strings?

Which was basically what she wanted, too.

So why was she driving away from him?

She turned at the light and went around several blocks until she finally found the disgusting house again. Charlie was sitting on the front steps, hands between his knees.

Bella got out of the car, feeling sheepish. "I guess I sort of got the wrong idea back there. I'm sorry," she told him, just as a cab pulled up behind her car.

"Stay right here," Charlie ordered, pointing at the step. "Sit. Please."

She did, and he loped over to the cab, said something to the driver and tried to give him some money. The driver threw the bills back at Charlie, swore, and then the cab screeched away down the street.

Charlie shrugged, picked up his money and came over and sat down beside Bella.

"What was his problem?"

"Who knows? I guess he thought he was getting a twenty-dollar fare, and was insulted when I handed him five and told him I didn't need him."

"Five dollars is five dollars. He must be doing pretty well to chuck money away." Catch her doing that.

"Whatever I said that made you mad, I'm sorry, Bella. I'm probably not thinking too straight. See, Alice tried to kill herself on Sunday night—she took a couple bottles of pills, and I've been at the hospital a lot."

"That's horrible. Is she okay?"

"Yeah. She's in the psych ward. They're keeping her for another few days. It's a good thing in disguise, because she's been depressed for a long time and now she'll get the counseling she needs."

"How's Emma holding up?"

He blew out a breath and shook his head. "She worries me. She figures it's her job in life to take care of her mother."

Bella was watching him. "Because you're not there to do it anymore?"

"Something like that." He gave her a rueful

smile, and she thought of Josh and his attitude around Oscar. There was an important message here—she'd make sure that Josh didn't feel he had to protect her.

"Why didn't you tell me earlier about Alice?" Now that annoyed her. "I mean about my kids, my devious mother, my on-again off-again father, not to mention my absentee good-for-nothing husband. And you don't say a word when a big, bad thing happens to your family?"

He looked down at the step. "I guess I just figured you have enough on your plate, without me heaping my problems on top."

"Friends talk, and friends confide in each other, Charlie." She blew out a breath. "So forget the friendship aspect and let's talk sex. According to our last conversation, I'm just supposed to get naked, say nothing except Oh, God, Oh, God, and then get dressed and we go our separate ways? Because that's what it sounds like you want."

He looked surprised. "Well, I really hope the Oh, God part works. Seeing that the responsibility for it lies with me."

"Oh, yeah? Since when? Last I heard, it was up to both parties involved. Niki gave me a long lecture on it when we were about sixteen. And going back again to the previous conversation, when we were discussing friendship, I'm pretty steamed about you keeping quiet. Not confiding in me suggests a lack of trust."

"It won't happen again. Promise."

"Cross your heart and hope to die."

He did. Bella laughed, and the tension was gone.

She glanced at her watch and got to her feet. "Time to head home. My prospective buyer is arriving at six and I have to shovel a path through the junk that's spread all over the house." She searched her bag and her pockets for her keys.

"They're here." Charlie reached in his pocket and handed them to her. "You set them on the steps and I didn't want to get left behind all over again."

"You, Charlie Fredricks, have a suspicious nature."

"More like practical. Think about it—I could get that same cab driver. He looked pretty dangerous to me."

"There is that." They got in the car, and when they'd gone a few blocks in silence, Charlie said, "So how are we going to do this?"

"This being…?" She didn't dare take her eyes off the road.

"This being the urge I have to do stuff like this." He reached over, lifted her T-shirt and jacket, bent down and nibbled at her belly.

She yelped and then shivered. "Charlie. For

God's sake, control yourself. I'm trying to drive here." She braked hard to keep from hitting the car ahead of her, and they both jerked forward against their seat belts.

"There's a bus beside us, for heaven's sake." She was scandalized. "They can see right in."

"So you're not into voyeurism. Okay, that's a good beginning. How about…" He slid his big, warm hand slowly up her denim-covered thigh, letting it come to rest with his thumb on her crotch. "They can't really see this, right?"

Bella began to quiver. "If you enjoy accidents, just keep this up, you maniac. What's got into you, anyway? First you give me a lecture about just being business partners, and then you try to seduce me in my own car."

"Ideas, Bella. I'm finding out I'm not a patient man. How long until your kids get home?"

Bella glanced at her watch. "A couple of hours. Kelsey has swimming. And Josh…"

"Is at basketball. So would you rather go to a hotel, have me come to your house or brave my apartment?"

She had trouble catching her breath. "A hotel would make me feel like a hooker. I guess I'd feel more comfortable at home. I'd rather you came over."

She tried to remember what her bedroom looked like. Not good. And she didn't want to be anywhere with him that she'd been with Gordon. There was the guest room—that shouldn't be too bad. Apart from the paint cans in the closet. But the bed was made up. At least she thought it was.

"This is the shortest route to your house, right?" His voice was low and urgent. He was stroking her in vulnerable areas, and then he leaned over and licked her neck.

"Guaranteed, it is." Her blood was pounding in her veins and she felt hot and wet and aroused beyond belief.

She pulled up in front of her house and turned into the driveway. A rusty green car painted with psychedelic yellow flowers blocked the garage. The back window was missing, there was a huge ding on the rear fender and the back bumper was held up with duct tape. Bella's heart sank. This couldn't be good.

"Friend of yours, Charlie?" How she hoped so. Bella opened her door, stepped out and stared at the hippie wagon.

"Nobody I know." He got out as well, just as Oscar came around the corner of the garage.

"*Bella mia.* I hope you don't mind me just dropping by like this, but I wanted to give you my new address. The phone isn't hooked up yet— they're coming on Friday." He walked over and patted the car, as if it were a puppy.

"And these are my new wheels."

Bella nodded, wondering how long he intended to stay. There was now only an hour and a half before the kids came home, and she felt painfully let down. "I tried to call you at the hotel, and they said you'd checked out."

"Sorry about that. I should have left word for you, but I happened to meet this guy who had a house and needed a roommate. His wife left him, and so I moved in with him. Baxter, his name is."

"And you got this car...where?" From the city dump, by the looks of the thing, Bella thought. "Does it run?" She had visions of it abandoned in her driveway, with potential buyers taking one look and deciding these weren't the people they wanted to buy a house from in such an upscale neighborhood.

"It needs a little work. It runs rough, but I can get it purring like a top in no time. Got it for nothing—how about that?"

Bella thought nothing was probably more than the car was worth.

Oscar was on a high. "Baxter has a friend who runs a sort of junk shop, and someone traded him the car for a couple of beds. I got it in return for working for him for a week. He wants to go fishing. Of course, the insurance was expensive."

Bella realized that Charlie had been standing back quietly during this whole conversation.

She sighed and remembered her manners.

"Charlie Fredricks, this is my father, Oscar Howard."

Charlie stepped forward and extended his hand. "Pleased to meet you, Oscar."

"Likewise." Oscar gave Charlie's hand a hefty shake. "You got a good firm grip there, young fella."

Charlie asked what Bella had been wondering. "How did you get the car through the testing station?" In order to get insurance, a car had to pass stringent rules that covered brakes, emissions and general road fitness.

"Baxter got it passed—some friend of his works at the place. It's actually in better shape than it looks."

It would have to be, Bella thought, because it looked like it belonged on a junk heap. For a few moments everyone stood around awkwardly in the driveway without saying anything. Oscar didn't make any move to leave. It started to rain again, and Bella couldn't stand the tension or the drizzle an instant longer. She caved.

"Do you want to come in, Dad? Charlie?"

Charlie nodded and sighed, and Oscar smiled at her.

"Now that's kind of you, Bella. I'd really like to see my grandkids again, if it's okay by you." He started toward the front door, and Bella shrugged and shook her head hopelessly at Charlie.

There went her hour-and-a-half window. There went her chances at an orgasm in the immediate future. Probably for the foreseeable future, considering how her life was going. By the slump of Charlie's shoulders, Bella figured he was probably feeling much the same.

In the kitchen, Bella made tea, and they were sitting drinking it when Mae used her key to the front door.

"Annabella? Whose disgusting old car is that in your driveway? Because it really doesn't give a very good first impression…."

She rounded the corner, looking first at Charlie. Then her gaze went to Oscar, and her mouth dropped open.

She shut it with an audible click and her face turned magenta.

"*You? Oscar Howard!* What in heaven's name are *you* doing here?"

"Visiting my family. What's it look like?"

Bella stared at her father. So he had a snappy side to him.

Mae puffed up like a wind sock in a gale. "How dare you show your face after what you did? You don't deserve a family, running off with that whore of yours, deserting me and Annabella."

"Just hold on a second, woman." Oscar's voice got louder and he stood up. "I sent money!" He punctuated each word with a fist thumped on the counter. Tea cups slopped and the spoons rattled.

"I sent letters and plane tickets—and you sent them all back. You lied to Bella, letting her think I didn't care about her." He was hollering by now. "You've got a lot to answer for, Mae Collins."

"It's still Howard, you old nincompoop. If Annabella had to use your name, I couldn't let her do it alone. So now the whole thing's *my* fault. If that isn't just like you, you cheating, lying deserter. You never could take responsibility for anything. Least of all yourself."

Bella noticed that Mae didn't deny anything, though. She had her wind back, and she was on the defensive.

"*You* were the one who lied and cheated and left us, Oscar Howard." Mae marched over to him, until they were nearly nose to nose. "You walked out on us and took every last cent we had and spent it on that…that floozy. I even had to go to welfare and ask for enough money to get us through until I could find a job."

Bella had never heard that. She doubted it was true.

"I left you most of what we had. But we didn't *have* much, because you went through it like water. Remember the piano?"

The piano? Bella sure as heck didn't remember any piano.

"I wanted our daughter to have music lessons."

"So you bought a grand piano? It didn't even fit in the living room. As for spending money on the woman I loved, it was Dinah who bought the plane tickets and not me."

"Oh, piffle. You bailed on us, you coward. Now get out of here and take your pile-of-junk car with you." Mae had obviously forgotten it was Bella's house they were in. "And don't you even speak that woman's name again in my presence."

"Dinah, Dinah, Dinah," Oscar chanted like an annoying three-year-old.

"Enough." Bella was on her feet, and her raised voice outdid both of them. "Go somewhere else to wash your old laundry, both of you. My kids are coming home any minute, and I don't want them walking into this."

"It's not me," Oscar said, leveling a finger at Mae. "It's her fault—"

"It's him," Mae all but shrieked. "He's a liar and a coward and a womanizer and—"

"Grandpa?" No one had heard Kelsey come in. "Nana? Oh, hi, Charlie. Wow, like, *everybody's* here, right?"

She sounded artificially upbeat, poor kid. She had to have heard the hollering match, Bella realized. One thing about it, her kids weren't going to be lacking material to relate to their counselors later in life.

Both of Bella's parental units looked shame-faced, to give them credit they didn't deserve.

And of course it was Mae who recovered first. The woman was tougher than any old shoe Bella had ever come across.

"I dropped by to take you shopping, Kelsey," she said in a tensely cheery voice. "There's a sale at Sears. I thought we could look at coats, and eat at the lunch counter."

"Whose wild ride is that in the drive?" Josh was right behind his sister.

"Mine," Oscar said. "I wanted to ask your mom if maybe you could come out with me for an hour or two. Get a burger or something."

"Can I?" Josh asked Bella.

Kelsey chimed in. "And can I go with Nana?"

About to deny everyone everything, Bella glanced over at Charlie. The naked longing on his face reminded her of what they'd had planned for that afternoon, and she changed her mind.

Sure, she had serious doubts about letting Josh near Oscar's wreck of a car, but what could it do except stall? It wasn't as if they were taking it on the highway.

And her mother was undoubtedly going to try to turn Kelsey against her grandfather, but Kelsey was a smart kid. Bella had faith that her daughter wouldn't swallow anything without questioning it thoroughly.

"Go," she said to them both. Lust was no respecter of motherhood. "Just go."

When the door closed behind children and parents, she snapped the lock in place, closed her eyes and took several calming breaths, and then grabbed Charlie's hand and hurried him up the stairs to the spare bedroom.

CHAPTER TWELVE

HALF AN HOUR LATER, Bella decided that either the man was exceptionally gifted, or her experience with sex had been limited to the marital kind for far too long. She'd never dreamed she was multiorgasmic.

"You smell so good," Charlie murmured, trailing kisses down her neck and across her collarbone. "And you're soft, so soft all over."

"Except for my heels," she babbled, shivering as his mouth found her left nipple. Why hadn't she rasped away the dead skin on her heels and rubbed on Vaseline or something? And she hadn't shaved her legs, either. But her careless grooming didn't seem to be too much of a problem for him. He was making soft, growling noises that any idiot would realize meant he was having at least as much fun as she was.

"You're so good…" She caught her breath as he did something creative with his tongue. "So good at this. At all of it. But especially the, Oh, my

God, Charlie, the kissing." His lips were near her navel and heading south. And soon her breathing deteriorated into gasps and, at one magnificent juncture, a long declaration of approval.

He'd even brought condoms. Niki had told Bella to stock up on them, and she'd told her which store to go to because they had some special sheepskin kind, but of course Bella hadn't. That conversation had occurred just after Gordon left.

But now she was looking at Charlie, and taking everything in. She'd sneaked a quick look back at the beginning, and Charlie's hadn't seemed so much out of the ordinary.

And technique wasn't really it, either. Technique suggested a set of A's and B's and a chart. The thing about Charlie—the thing that made her lose her breath and turn to mush inside—was his enthusiasm for the job at hand, his total dedication to making her happy, his innovative approach. She didn't doubt for an instant that he loved what he was doing, and what he was doing was making her wish they had the entire evening instead of just—

"Oh, no! What time is it?" She reached out and groped for his watch, which was under the pillow. Had been under the pillow.

"The people who want to look at the house. They're coming at…" She found the watch under his left hip, squinted at it, and went into a frenzy, trying to disentangle herself from his arm and right leg.

"They'll be here in twenty minutes." She scrambled off the bed and tried to find her underwear. "We've got to tidy up. What if they're early?"

The doorbell chimed.

"They're early," she shrieked. "Everything's a mess. What am I going to do?"

Charlie bolted up and pulled on his pants, not bothering about underwear.

"I'll go and stall them," he said, tugging on his shirt. "You do what you can in five minutes."

It took twelve, but she managed to get into her clothes, splash her face in the bathroom, respike her hair and kick things under beds, as she tore from one room to the next, swearing.

Still vibrating from the aftermath of vigorous sex and frantic tidying, she took one shaky breath and started down the stairs. She could hear Charlie extolling the virtues of the kitchen, and she plastered on a smile as she rounded the corner.

"Bella," he said with a smile that mirrored hers, "you spoke to Harry Schulman on the phone? And this is his wife, Marlena. Marlena, this is Bella Monroe."

Marlena was six feet tall and stunning. Her voice suggested adenoids and tone deafness, however. She whined, "Is there a built-in water purifier with the refrigerator?"

"Actually, no," Bella said, taking in the other

woman's designer track suit and hoping that the stains on her own jeans didn't show too much. "I use a Brita filter."

"Is there under-floor heating in the bathrooms? And what about air filters? Our children are so allergic, aren't they, Harry?" She pointed at the hallway carpeting. "I assume there's hardwood under there? Because of course we'll have to rip out all the carpets and have the floors redone. Carpeting is so unhygienic, with mites and so forth." She opened the fridge and stared at the contents, milk past its expiry date, badly wrapped leftovers, half-empty bottles of ketchup and mustard. Yogurt had spilled onto the top rack.

"Goodness," Marlena said. She closed the fridge gently and opened the oven, where several things had overflowed and left blackened charcoal lumps. "It *is* self-cleaning, right?"

"Right. But apparently you do have to turn it on." Bella was losing hope for any sale. She was also beginning to intensely dislike Marlena, who was now opening and closing her cupboards.

"We don't eat any processed food," the woman said, taking in Bella's hoarded stock of emergency rations—tins of soup and boxes of things that needed water added and five minutes in the microwave. "All those nitrites are so damaging to children's growing bodies."

"Actually, the food doesn't go with the house,"

Bella cooed. A second too late she caught Charlie's warning glance.

He said, "Why don't I show you around upstairs? You'll love the view from the master bedroom—you can see right out to Pacific Spirits Park. And look at this staircase. Very few newer homes have these gracious stairways."

He'd forgotten "elegant." Bella clenched her fists and followed behind, taking comfort from Harry's broad beam. Judging from the size of it, the poor man probably sneaked fast food when Dragon Lady wasn't looking.

Charlie outdid himself pointing out the new paint job, the high ceilings, the expensive wainscoting.

Bella—and without a doubt, Marlena—noticed the smell of old sneakers in Josh's room, the burn mark on the carpet, the spilled navy nail polish on the duvet in Kelsey's room, and—lord have mercy—the sight of Charlie's navy-blue jockey shorts peeking out from under the bed in the spare bedroom.

She'd jerked the duvet up over the sheets, but somehow she'd missed the underwear.

That was when Bella left all hope behind, scuttled back downstairs and collapsed on the sofa. She could hear Charlie valiantly chattering on with his sales pitch, but Bella didn't move when the Schulmans, trailed by Charlie, came down again. Fortunately, they went straight to the front door.

"We'll be in touch," Harry lied. Marlena was already halfway down the new sidewalk. Bella peeked through the living-room window. The woman seemed to be doing some sort of yoga exercise, swinging her arms up and over her head, holding them there for a second, and then lowering them. It sort of looked like a victory salute, but it probably meant she was getting rid of something nasty she'd picked up in Bella's unhygienic, nitrite-laden, sex-crazed home.

Charlie came into the living room and lowered himself to the sofa beside Bella. He blew out a long breath. "Holy shit," he said softly. "My knees are still shaking."

"Yeah. Mine, too. That went really well, don't you think?"

He gave her a look. "Joke, right? Marlena asked me if she could have a peek in the attic. Where the hell is the attic access?"

"How would I know? I've never been up there—you know I store all my leftover junk in the garage."

"She mentioned that. Apparently they glanced in there before they rang the doorbell. And there's about two dozen cans of paint in the bedroom closet. Did you know that?"

"Yeah. Isn't that trespassing? Can people do that—look in your closets and your garage and your fridge and your cupboards? Did she open the drawers in my bedroom and go through my under-wear?"

"No, but she poked in the closet."

"Bitch."

"Yeah. I should have grabbed my shorts. Sorry about that."

"It wouldn't have made any difference. She didn't like the house even before she went up-stairs—that was pretty obvious."

"They might still make an offer." But he didn't sound terribly hopeful. "It's liable to be low, though, so be prepared. Sometimes people try to get property that's for sale by the owner for way below market value, and then they turn around and resell it for profit. There was something about those two that didn't ring true to me."

"There was something about those two that made me want to be sick."

All the postcoital bliss that she'd been able to enjoy for about five seconds was gone. In its place was the familiar feeling of utter desperation. The money from Oscar would last about another week, at most.

"You'll have to expect a lot more potential buyers like them," Charlie warned, resting his head on the sofa back. "You'll probably get a lot of casual looks before you get a buyer. And they'll all try to get the price down, if they figure out you need money."

Bella got to her feet and began to pace up and down. "I do. Need money. Fast."

He watched her. "Just don't let them know that."

Bella stopped in front of him, hands on her hips. "But how long does it usually take, Charlie? For a house like this to sell?"

He shrugged. "Selling any house doesn't happen overnight, especially selling it yourself. It wouldn't hurt to do some advertising. Just having a sign on the curb doesn't attract many potential buyers—the only people who see it are the ones driving by. Most people go straight to the real-estate supplement in the paper, to see what's out there. Or the Internet."

Bella thought about that for a minute. "How much would an ad in the real-estate paper cost?"

"*Real Estate Weekly* doesn't run private ads, it's put out by the Greater Vancouver Real Estate Association. Naturally, they don't want people selling properties on their own. In a daily paper, an ad would run you maybe four or five hundred. For three days. You're looking at a limited audience. Serious buyers don't go to the classifieds if they're looking for a house."

Bella's desperation grew. "What you're telling me is that it's going to be really hard to sell this place myself."

It was exactly what all the real-estate people had warned. She hated the idea that they might have been right.

"I don't know that for sure." Charlie got up. "Could we maybe talk about this in the kitchen over coffee? I'm feeling a little wasted and a shot of caffeine might get me going again."

"I could use a shot of something myself." She put the coffee on and Charlie got the cream out of the fridge. Then Bella went over to him and put her arms around his chest. He held her tight.

"I'm scared, Charlie." Confessing it helped a little.

He hugged her even closer. "I'll give you all the help I can. I want this to work for you. If I had any money, I'd give you that, too, but at this moment, my finances and yours are a good match."

She clung to him. "Tell me this, honestly. Do you think I'd have a better chance of selling this place faster if I listed with an agent?"

He hesitated. "I can't say that for sure. You'd definitely get better coverage, and you wouldn't have to deal with people like the Schulmans. You'd be warned ahead of time when the house was to be shown, and the Realtor would walk prospective buyers through. You'd go out for coffee. Or wherever."

She disentangled herself and sat down across from him at the island, stirring cream into her mug.

"I could go out before they even got here?"

"That's easiest and it's usually best."

"What if I gave you the listing, Charlie? Exclusive, isn't that what they call it?"

"Yeah." He set his cup down. "But is that something you really want to do?"

"I think so. I feel overwhelmed and don't think I can do a good job of showing the house. And advertising—I guess I didn't give that enough thought. It sounds as though I'd spend a ton of money and probably not get great results."

"Why don't you think about it for a while? Make sure it's what you want?"

She leaned across the island. "Charlie, listen to me. *I don't have time to ponder over things.* I want you to sell this place. Now, are you agreeable or not?"

"Only if we make a deal over the commission. A half-and-half split, just between us."

"Sounds okay to me."

"I'll draw up a contract."

"When?"

"First thing in the morning." He got up and put his cup in the dishwasher. "I'll go to the office and pick one up. Then I'll bring it by…" He glanced at his watch and grimaced. "Damn, Bella, I have to go now. I said I'd stop at the hospital. I promised Emma. I'll come first thing in the morning, so you can look over the fine print, if that's okay." He stood up, went to the door, retrieved his shoes. He put them on and found his coat in the closet.

"Morning's fine. Thanks, Charlie." She kissed him as fervently as he kissed her, and then he held her close for several moments before he left.

HE'D GOTTEN THE LISTING. Charlie unlocked his truck and climbed in. So why did he feel totally rotten about it? He hadn't known the Schulmans would turn up, or that they'd be the kind of objectionable people they were. What he'd told Bella about advertising was absolutely true, and someone had undoubtedly told her the same things before; but she probably hadn't been listening.

He thought about how it had been, making love to her, and tenderness overwhelmed him. They'd been great together. He wanted them to be great together again, as soon as he could get her alone, as many times as he could get her alone, which was no job for the fainthearted. As far as he knew, there weren't any hard-and-fast rules about sleeping with a client before she became a client. And he sure as hell hadn't made out with her just to get the listing, that was certain. As if that would work with Bella, anyhow.

He'd do a first-class job for her. She'd likely get a little less for the house, what with commission, but with the split he'd offered, the differential wouldn't be great. And he'd bust his butt to get her a quick sale.

So why did he feel so terrible?

CHAPTER THIRTEEN

BELLA CLOSED THE DOOR behind him. The relief of having the sale out of her hands was huge. She went and got her harmonica, and was rendering a fair approximation of "Love Me Do" when Mae and Kelsey got home.

Mae scowled at the harmonica. "I didn't know you had one of those things, Annabella."

"Dad used to play one, remember?" There were lots of things she wanted her mother to remember, but not in front of Kelsey. Bella smiled at her daughter. "So, you two had a good time?"

"Awesome, Mom. Nana bought me this cashmere scarf *and* a new coat," Kelsey chirped. She took off her jacket and emptied two boxes on the table. She pulled on a puffy, ankle-length purple coat and looped a multicolored, mile-long scarf around her throat. "Aren't they great?"

They were, but Bella still gave her mother a pointed look. How many times had she asked Mae to consult her before any major clothing items were purchased?

"I should really be getting home." Her guilty eyes darted here and there, never quite meeting Bella's gaze.

"Not so fast. Take your coat off, Mother. I have some things to talk over with you. Privately." Bella said, "Kelsey, I'd like you to do a major cleanup on that bedroom of yours. Hang up your clothes and vacuum. And check under the bed—half your wardrobe was on the floor when some people came to look at the house."

Mae would call this locking the barn after the horse was stolen, but Bella was in no mood for aphorisms.

"Mom!" Kelsey whined. "You sure know how to spoil a great day." She headed up the stairs in slow motion, trailing her scarf behind her.

Mae slowly removed her coat, setting it on a chair, telegraphing the message that she wouldn't be staying long. Under any other circumstances, Bella would have been relieved. But tonight she wanted Mae around for a while. They had issues to discuss.

When Kelsey was safely out of earshot, Bella retrieved the letters Oscar had given her. She was trembling when she set them on the island.

"These are letters from my father, Mom. Why did you send them back? They weren't even addressed to you. You had no right to deny me contact with him."

Mae touched one of the envelopes with a stiff

finger. As if it were poisoned, she rubbed her hand on her pants and then patted her heart with her palm. "I was protecting you. How can you even let that man in your house, Annabella?"

"You lied to me. You didn't tell me he'd ever phoned, and you sent all my letters back. He even wanted me to fly down to Florida and see him, and you refused without asking me what I wanted. How could you do that, Mae? How could you be so dishonest?"

"Me, dishonest? That's ridiculous. All I was doing was saving you from more heartache, Annabella. As if I'd ever expose you to that awful woman. Lord only knows what kind of depravity they got up to in Florida."

"She was sick, Mom. I doubt there was much X-rated stuff going down. No, it wasn't that. What you were doing was cutting me off from my father." Bella was so angry she was suddenly speechless. She had to stop and take a couple shaky breaths before she could continue. "You know what Kelsey's like about Gordon—she needs to believe he's coming back. Whether he is or not, I'd brain anyone who took that hope away from her. The way you did to me."

Mae's face was scarlet, and her hand was patting her chest so fast it looked like a humming-bird's wing. "He was no father to you—" she began, but Bella cut her off.

"Yes, he was. He was the only father I had."
Tears filled Bella's eyes, and she brushed them
away. "He used to take me fishing. He taught me
to swim and play checkers. He would play songs
for me on the harmonica, and when I was little I'd
dance for him. Regardless of what went on between the two of you, *I loved him*.

"You knew that. And you were jealous, Mae."
Bella slammed a hand down on top of the letters.
"*That's* what sending these back was really all
about."

Mae's lips quivered and she shook her head
vehemently.

"Not jealous, Bella, never that. No, I was scared
for you," she whispered. "I was scared you'd get
hurt even more. I couldn't stand you being hurt the
way I was. Trusting him, loving him with all your
heart, and then being betrayed."

Bella stared at her mother. Mae had never
before admitted she'd once been in love with
Oscar.

"How did you meet him, Mom?" She'd never
dared ask before, because any mention of him sent
Mae into a rant.

Not this time. She said in a quiet tone, "I was
working at Fleming's Drugs, over on Main Street.
Oscar was doing construction work, putting in a
new sewer pipe in the alley, and he cut his hand. I
put antiseptic on it and bandaged it for him, and

he asked me out to a movie. Gary Cooper was in it, some cowboy thing. We went to the White Spot for a burger afterward. We went on seeing each other, and three months later he asked me to marry him. I've always regretted not getting to know him better first. I didn't know what kind of man he really was. But I wanted to get married and raise a family."

And hadn't that been one of the reasons Bella had married Gordon? That deep-seated need to make a home, have children and live happily ever after? She'd always thought she and Mae were as different as two people could be, but now she saw clearly they'd made similar choices—and ended up in similar circumstances.

"I'm sorry, Mom." Bella reached over and took her hand. "I'm sorry it didn't work out for you, either."

Before Mae could reply, they heard Josh's voice, raised with excitement. He was talking to Oscar as they came through the door. "And then, Gramps, you would not *believe* what happened…."

"I will not be in the same room with *him*." Mae pulled away from Bella, snatched up her coat and jammed her arms into the sleeves as Oscar and Josh came into the kitchen.

And just like that, the moment she'd shared with her mother was gone. Mae was back to her usual self, but at least Bella knew there was more behind the harsh, accusing tone than she'd ever suspected.

"Hi, Nana." Josh's voice was tentative, and he shot an anxious, guilty glance at Oscar that told Bella her father had said something not very nice to him about Mae.

Turning to Bella, Josh said, "Gramp's car is way cool, Mom. He's gonna teach me how to drive it, so I can get my license."

"Humph." Mae's snort was loud. "That car is not safe. Your father would never allow you to even get into that wreck, Josh."

"Yeah, well, my father's not here, is he?" The remark was mildly insolent, and Bella cautioned him.

"Josh. Who do you think you're speaking to?"

"Sorry," he mumbled in Mae's direction. "I can, though, right, Mom? Learn to drive? Gramps promised."

"We'll see." Bella was now irritated with her father. What did he think he was doing, promising Josh driving lessons without so much as mentioning it to her first?

"Josh, don't you have homework? Go up now and start it, I'd like a private word with your nana and grandpa."

He started to argue, then took a look at Bella's expression and gave in gracefully. "Okay. Night, Nana. Thanks, Gramps. I had a great time."

The moment he was gone the bickering began, before Bella had a chance to gather her thoughts and say anything to them.

"You have your nerve, showing your face around here after all this time," Mae sniped.

"Far as I know, it's a free country," Oscar snarled. "And I have a right to visit my grandchildren."

"You don't deserve grandchildren," Mae hissed. "You deserted them along with the rest of us. They're teenagers now, and they don't even know you."

"They will. I intend to be around awhile."

"So where's your fancy woman, Oscar? You walk out on her, too?"

"Dinah passed away, and I'll thank you not to speak ill of her. She was a real woman, not some dried up, frigid—"

"*Stop it.*" Bella was in shock. The nastiness these two displayed was far worse than the worst quarrel she and Gordon had ever had.

Tears began to roll down her cheeks. It hurt her to think that they were her parents, these vicious, blame-throwing senior citizens. She must have blocked out the memory of their quarrels, overheard when she was a little girl. There was a sick feeling in the pit of her belly. Had her kids felt like this, overhearing their parents fights? If they had, she had some apologies to make.

"Dad, you have no right to make promises to Josh, without asking me first. And Mom, I've told you before about buying expensive clothing for Kelsey without my permission."

"Oh, honestly, Annabella, your *permission*," Mae began. "I'm her nana, I have a right to spoil her."

It was the argument that had always silenced Bella's objections.

Not this time. "They're my children and I make the rules. I have to—I'm the only parent they have at the moment." She drew a shuddering breath, and what came out of her mouth surprised even her. "And the first rule is, neither of you is welcome here again until you make peace between yourselves."

CHAPTER FOURTEEN

THEY LOOKED EQUALLY shocked—and equally outraged.

"But that's not fair," Mae warbled. "You can't
stop me from seeing my grandchildren."

"Yes, I can," Bella said. She kept her voice low
and controlled. "I don't want either of you around
Kelsey or Josh again, unless you can be civil to one
another. Not just in this house, either. I won't have
you taking the kids out and then running each
other down when I'm not listening."

Oscar seemed abashed.

Bella leveled a look at Mae. "The way you did
after Dad left, Mom. It's hurtful and it forces them
to take sides, when it's not their affair."

Mae harrumphed as she buttoned up her coat.
"You'll be sorry, Annabella. Those children need
their nana. And just remember, when you need
money, it's not *him* you'll get it from." She jerked
a disdainful thumb at Oscar.

"Actually, Dad gave me some money. And I

have a check right here for you." Bella had written it earlier. She dug it out of her handbag and held it out to Mae. "I appreciate the loan, but I'm fine now." Such a lie, but necessary.

"But you haven't sold the house yet—you'll need it." Mae actually appeared frightened, and Bella almost caved. But the quarrel still hung in the air, and the letters Mae had prevented her from seeing were on the table.

"Charlie's taking care of that for me."

"Well, I never. If *that's* how you feel…" Mae snatched the check and stuffed it in her bag. "I'll be going, then."

She hesitated, obviously expecting Bella to call her back. When the door closed behind her Oscar was still standing by the kitchen island, a hangdog look on his lined face. "You can't mean that, *Bella mia*. About me not seeing Josh and Kelsey?"

"Actually, I do. Unless you and Mae work out some sort of truce between you, I don't want either of you around the kids."

"But it's Mae's fault—"

"I don't want to hear it." Bella went to the closet and got his coat. "When, and if, you and Mae can speak to one another in a civil fashion and act like adults, then you both can see the kids as much as you want. Let me know when that happens."

Which would be about the twelfth of never, she guessed, watching Oscar walk down the front

sidewalk, feet dragging. Uncertainty gripped her.
Was she making a terrible mistake by denying her
children contact with their grandparents? God
knew, they had few enough relatives. But Josh and
Kelsey didn't need to be in the middle of a war
zone, either.

She thought of calling Charlie and talking
over her decision with him, but he'd said he was
going to the hospital. She thought of the lovemaking they'd shared, and she shivered. Already, she wanted more. And yet she knew it
wouldn't be smart to become too dependent on
him, sexually or any other way. He's spelled out
what he wanted from her, and it wasn't happily
ever after.

They were business partners. He was going to
sell her house. So they were part-time lovers—
that didn't mean they had a relationship. It didn't
mean she had the right to dump her domestic
problems on him, even though she'd done so
often enough.

*Get it through your head, Bella. The man is re-
lationshipped out, what with Emma and Alice.
And you—look at you. Two kids, impossible
parents, missing husband, missing car, a pile of
debts. A big prize you are.*

But she had to tell someone, just for the
pleasure of saying Charlie's name.

She made dinner, waited until the kids were

asleep and then dialed the familiar number of her best friend, eager to tell all.

"Niki? Hey, how's it going?"

"Oh, Bel... Bella." Her voice broke.

"What's wrong?" Bella got to her feet, gripping the receiver.

Niki was crying, which she never did. Bella's heart began to race, and fear made her cold.

Her friend sniffled, and then said, "Bella, geez, you won't believe this. I had to wait until I was sure, and I am—at least I think I'm, pretty sure. The doctor says so." Her voice broke again. "I'm...I'm pregnant!"

"Oh, Niki, that's the best news ever! I'm so happy for you. How far along are you?"

"Eight weeks. I just missed my second period. I'm almost scared to even hope, Bella."

Bella wiped moisture from her eyes. It was the closest thing to a miracle she'd encountered in a very long time.

"Niki, you'd be the first one to say how crazy that is. Just enjoy it. How's Tom taking it?"

"He's right here beside me, listening to me babble." Niki giggled, but there was a catch in her voice. "He's treating me like I'm gonna break, can you believe it? Me, with calves of steel and muscles like Popeye from wrestling hair all day." Her voice changed. "He really wants this, Bella. We both do. So much it's scary."

"Don't be scared. Just be grateful and happy. I'm gonna hang up now, so you two can celebrate."

"I'm trying to convince him it's okay to fool around, but he's a hard sell," Niki said with a wicked giggle that sounded more like her. "He'll be even harder in a minute, though. Talk to you later."

Bella hung up slowly. Niki, pregnant. She was elated for her friend. She'd waited so long for this, tried so hard.

With a pang of nostalgia, Bella remembered how it had felt, being pregnant with her own beloved babies, first Josh and then Kelsey. Gordon hadn't been overjoyed either time. She'd been the one who'd most wanted a family. What would it be like to be with someone who adored you, as Tom did Niki? Who wanted for you everything you wanted for yourself?

Charlie had said he wanted things to work for her. He'd said that if he had money, he'd give it to her. And he'd also indicated pretty clearly that he didn't want any future with her.

She thought of him in bed, again, and allowed herself to wonder exactly how he'd reacted when Alice told him she was going to have his baby. The way a man reacted to news like that said an awful lot about what sort of man he really was.

She decided she'd ask him. Casually. When the opportunity presented itself.

THE NEXT MORNING, Charlie stopped by the office to pick up Bella's contract and borrow a camera to take some photos for advertising.

"You got the listing?" Rick pounded him on the shoulder. "Way to go, little bro," he crowed. "I'm gonna make serious money on this one. The pool had sizable odds against you, but I had faith."

Janice Feldergast, the only female Realtor in the office, came in at that moment. "What's all the hollering about?"

"Charlie got the FSBO in Shaughnessy."

"Wow, congratulations." Her tone bordered on snide. "Didn't have to trade your body for the listing, I hope?"

"Nothing so drastic," Charlie replied, feeling more than ever like a traitor.

"You'll have to let us know what finally worked," she said with a wink. "So we can use it."

"Honesty," Charlie stated, wishing it was so.

"Whatever it was, you won the bonus, Charlie boy," Rick told him.

"Put it against what I owe you." He picked up the camera and hurried out.

At Bella's, he meticulously took her through every single clause in the agreement.

"Cease and desist, already," she moaned. "Just

let me sign the damn thing. Then we should load up supplies and go over to that horrible house and start trying to repair it."

"Did you happen to ask Oscar if he wants to work with us?"

"No. I was too busy laying down the law." She explained that she'd told Oscar and Mae they'd have to make peace between themselves if they wanted to see the kids. "Do you think that's unreasonable?" she asked anxiously.

"Nope. It sounds practical. Otherwise you've got each of them trying to get the kids on their side of an argument that's way older than they are."

"That's how I see it, too. Thanks for the support."

"Any time."

"How's Alice?"

"They're releasing her today and I have to go pick her up later. She's getting psychiatric help. Emma's in group therapy. I'm trying to convince myself I'm not the reason for my entire family being bonkers."

"Don't be ridiculous. You don't have that much power."

"You really know how to hurt a guy." Charlie reached out and pulled Bella into his arms. He couldn't help it.

She licked his ear. "The kids are in school. We could go upstairs before we head over to the bomb site. Just to fortify ourselves."

"Funny, I was thinking that. You're sexy as hell, you know that?"

"Thank you." She smiled at him. "You're pretty hot yourself."

He was kissing her neck, holding her bottom cupped in his hands and pressed tight against his groin, when Kelsey walked in.

OVER CHARLIE'S SHOULDER, Bella caught a glimpse of her daughter's horrified face. She pulled free from Charlie's arms as Kelsey turned and ran, wrenching the back door open and pelting through it, leaving it wide-open behind her.

"Kelsey." Bella ran after her, through the back door and down the steps. "Kelsey, wait. Stop."

She had made it only as far as the garage. She was slumped down, crouched in a tight ball, back against the wall, arms over her head. Her sobs tore a hole in Bella's heart.

"Sweetheart." Bella knelt beside her, putting out a hand to touch her arm. "Oh, Kelsey."

"Get away from me." Her daughter swung and caught Bella a glancing blow on her shoulder. "Get away from me, you—you *pig!* How could you let him kiss you? Are you sleeping with him? You are, aren't you? What about my daddy?" Sobs overcame her.

"Kelsey, please." Guilty, miserable and desperate, Bella tried to pull the girl to her feet, but

Kelsey resisted. "Come in the house, and we'll talk about it."

"I'm not coming in as long as *he's* in there."

"Okay. I'll tell him we need to be alone. But please come in the house."

She shook her head hard. "When he's gone." Kelsey wrapped her arms around herself, shaking off Bella's hand.

With an anxious glance back at her daughter, Bella hurried into the house. Charlie was waiting at the door, looking as upset as she felt.

He said, "Is there anything I can do?"

"She won't come in as long as you're here."

"Bella, I'm sorry this happened. Damn it. Can I talk to her?"

Bella shook her head. "It wouldn't help right now. She's pretty upset. She's never given up believing her father's coming back."

"Yeah, I know. That's a tough one. I'll leave, but call me and tell me how things are going, will you?"

Bella nodded. She heard his truck start, and after he'd driven away, Kelsey came in. Not looking up, she headed for the stairs, but Bella stopped her, taking her arm.

"Come and sit down, Kelsey."

The girl tried to wrench away, but Bella hung on.

"No. Let me go, Mother. I don't want to talk to you."

"Well, that's too bad, because we're going to talk, anyway." Bella steered them to the kitchen stools. "Sit down. I'll make us some tea. How come you're not in school?"

"I…I got my period." She hiccupped. "I threw up and I have cramps. The health nurse drove me home."

Why hadn't the woman called first? But there was no point in blaming someone else. Bella poured boiling water over teabags, added sugar and handed one mug to Kelsey.

"How are you feeling now?" Stupid question.

"Sick. My belly hurts." Kelsey took a sip of tea. "I have a bad headache."

"Did the nurse give you anything for it?"

"No. She said she needs your permission to give me medication."

"This should help." Bella handed her an ibuprofen. "And take a hot bath, that'll help, too. I'll find the heating pad for you. We'll do all that in a minute, but first, Kelsey, about Charlie and me…"

The revulsion on her daughter's face was hard to take. "How could you do that?" she demanded. "How could you let him kiss you like that?"

It was tough, but it had to be said. "Honey, your father and I are separated. We will be getting a divorce." *If I can ever locate the rat to serve him the papers.* "I have a right to have adult friends."

"That wasn't being friends. That was, like, totally disgusting." She looked Bella in the eye, and there was challenge in her tone. "He won't be coming here anymore, right?"

"Wrong. Charlie is selling this house for us. And he and I are repairing those others I told you about. When they sell, I'll earn some money." *Which we desperately need.* "So, yes, he will be coming here again."

"Then I'll go live with Nana."

Shocked, taken entirely off guard, Bella was speechless for a moment.

"That's not an option, Kelsey," she said at last. "This is still a family, whether your father is here or not. You'll stay right here, with Josh and me. And when Charlie's around, you'll be polite to him."

"I don't have to." Kelsey's expression was mutinous. "Nana said I could live with her. She said I could move in anytime I wanted."

Was there any end to the hurting? It took control, but Bella kept her voice quiet and even. "Mae had no right to tell you that. I'm your mother, and I'll say where you live."

"Yeah, well, I hate you. I'd way rather live with Nana." She got up so quickly the stool overturned and crashed to the floor. Ignoring it, she stomped down the hall and up the stairs. Her bedroom door slammed, and Bella put her head down on the counter.

How had her life turned into this train wreck? And what was the penalty for murdering your mother?

CHAPTER FIFTEEN

AFTER LEAVING BELLA, Charlie headed back to the office. He wanted to publish a special ad in *Real Estate Weekly,* featuring Bella's house.

He felt anxious, concerned because Kelsey had seen him fondling her mother, but also worried because his personal situation with Bella was becoming more and more complicated.

After making love to her that first time, he couldn't be around her without wanting to do it again. And again. Just thinking about her excited him, the way her body responded to his, all that lovely, sleek slenderness, the way she made him laugh at unexpected moments. There was a tenderness to her, hidden beneath her smart mouth and irritable personality, that made him uncomfortably aware that having sex with her wasn't just a physical process. There was an emotional component. There was a deep desire to possess, to make her his in every respect.

Hold it, Fredricks. Where are you going with this?

Wherever it was, it scared the hell out of him.

Their lives were messy enough, what with children and ex-partners and money problems and extended family.

Speaking of which, Rick's car was in the parking lot when Charlie arrived. He didn't want to talk to Rick. He particularly didn't want to discuss Bella, or her house, or the agreement to sell. He still felt he'd been less than honest with her, and it wasn't a good feeling at all.

He walked in to find the door to Rick's office closed, which suited Charlie fine.

Lenora, the young receptionist, greeted him with a wide smile. "Hey, Charlie, congratulations on the listing."

"Thanks." He headed for an empty desk, already planning the glowing text that would go with the color photo of Bella's house.

"Charlie." The office door swung open and Rick stuck his head out. "Come on in here, there's someone who wants to say hello."

Reluctantly, Charlie got up and followed him into his spacious corner office.

Harry and Marlena Schulman were seated in Rick's leather chairs. "Hey, Charlie, how's it going?" Harry got up and extended his hand.

Marlena smiled at him.

Charlie's heart sank. These were the last two

people he wanted to see, and he suspected Rick was going to ask him to show them properties.

"How d'you do," he managed to murmur, taking the hand Harry offered and letting go as soon as possible.

Rick was expansive. "Sit down, Charlie. You want a coffee? I've got some of those new Colombian beans, they're something else." Rick had an all-in-one espresso machine, and loved to use it.

"No, thanks. Actually, I'm kind of busy. I'm doing up an exclusive for the *Weekly,* and I should get back to it."

"On the Shaughnessy property." His brother grinned knowingly.

"Yeah." Not hard to guess, because it was his only listing.

"We were just talking about that," Rick said. "These two did an admirable job, don't you think?"

Admirable? They'd been a major pain in the ass. Charlie frowned and shook his head. "Sorry, you've lost me."

Rick said, "On the look-see. I figured if your lady friend realized how rough it could be to show a home, she'd cave. And was I right, or was I right?"

"You mean you set that up?" Charlie was beginning to understand, and as it dawned on him what the score was, his blood pressure shot through the roof.

"You asked them to come by and look at the house?"

"Just a favor for a friend," Harry said with a toothy grin. "Last year Rick found us the apartment we'd always dreamed of, at a price that was nothing short of miraculous. I owed him one."

"Harry and I are golfing buddies. He regularly kicks my ass all over the green," Rick added, giving Harry a fond tap on the shoulder with his fist.

"And Marlena's an actress with Vancouver Little Theatre," Rick added. "I hear she put in an amazing performance as a picky buyer."

"Picky? I was downright obnoxious." Marlene's pleasant voice took on the whiny note Charlie remembered. "Is there a built-in water purifier with the fridge?"

Marlena and the two men laughed, and by the knowing looks and the snickers they all exchanged, Charlie guessed that his navy underwear was now general knowledge.

Trying to control his fury, he said, "I don't think that was very honest, Rick."

His brother was still laughing. "Oh, c'mon. All's fair in love and real estate, right? And it got you the listing. What more could you ask?"

Charlie walked out. It was either that or plant a fist on his brother's nose. He felt a little sick when he thought about Bella finding out that the Schulman thing had been a setup. To take his mind off that eventuality, he applied himself to concocting the best ad he could devise, and he didn't even glance up when the Schulmans left.

Rick followed them out, bantering with Harry. When they were gone, he came over to Charlie.

"What's with the attitude? You were downright rude in there." He leaned both hands on the desk, frowning. "Haven't you ever heard that the end justifies the means?"

Charlie stood up. He was a good head taller than Rick, and he used the fact now to his advantage. "Don't ever pull anything like that on me again." He kept his voice low, because Lenora was just a short distance away. "I'm grateful for all the help you've given me, but I don't intend to trick anyone into listing with me. *Ever*. And from here on in, stop treating me like the idiot sibling, because if there's much more of it, I'll rip your right arm off and stuff it up your ass. Got that?"

"You're pretty touchy." Rick scowled, but he also took two quick steps back. "What's happened to your sense of humor?"

"You might ask the same thing about your integrity, Rickie. Looks to me like anything goes with you, just to make a sale."

"Hey, you're the one screwing the client, not me."

It took every ounce of self-control Charlie possessed to keep from punching Rick. His brother must have realized how close he'd come, because he turned and zipped back into his office.

Janice Feldergast had come in at some point during the altercation. She didn't say anything at first, but Charlie could tell she'd overheard most of it, and certainly the part about screwing the client. Janice had made it very plain, not once but several times, that Charlie would be welcome in her bed, a suggestion he'd managed to deflect gracefully. Or so he'd thought.

After a few minutes she raised her eyebrows and gave him a knowing look. "Nasty job, but somebody's got to do it, eh, Charlie?"

He pretended not to know what she meant. "What job's that, Janice?"

She didn't answer, but the look she gave him sent a shiver down his spine.

He ignored her after that, pretending to apply himself to the ad as he tried to calm down.

After twenty minutes, Lenora said, "Phone for you, Charlie, online one."

It was Alice, and the moment he heard her voice he realized he'd totally forgotten about driving her home from the hospital.

"Charlie? Where are you?"

Her familiar whine brought familiar guilt and a rising sense of panic.

"I've been waiting and waiting for you, Charlie."

Codependent, the psychiatrist had said. Claire Sui's words echoed in his mind. "Alice, I apologize. I'm at work and I just forgot. Please call a cab, okay? I'll reimburse you for the fare."

"But you promised you'd be here, Charlie."

She wasn't going to let him off easy, but then she never had. "It was wrong of me to promise and then not show up. I'm sorry. It won't happen again."

"But it does, Charlie, all the time." She gave a heavy, beleaguered sigh. "You always say you'll do things and then you don't." She never got angry with him, and she didn't sound it now. She sounded martyred.

He made a decision.

"Not anymore, Alice. I'm going to stop promising things, as of right now. You'll have to make other arrangements when you want things done. It's time we both moved on with our lives. We need to be more independent. From now on, I intend to be."

There was a moment of silence. And then, in an aggrieved tone, she asked, "Are you saying you won't help me out anymore? You know I can't drive, Charlie. How will I get the things I need? How will I get to my appointments? Emma can't always come—she's in school. And there's so much to do at the house. Something's always breaking."

"Alice. You're a smart woman, and very capable. Take driving lessons and hire a handyman. Become independent, get a life of your own." The thing that bothered him the most came tumbling out. "Stop making our daughter responsible for you. It's not fair to her or to you. Can't you see what it's doing to her?" *To all of us,* he thought. *To your relatives, to the friends who've distanced themselves from you, to me, to Emma.*

Alice gave a choked sob and then hung up.

Charlie felt like a traitor. He dug in his wallet and found the number for Alice's doctor, relieved when she answered on the second ring. He told her exactly what he'd said.

"My timing was rotten, Claire. Now I'm afraid that Alice will do something again, take pills, cut her wrists—whatever. I shouldn't have said those things to her, not now, at any rate. Certainly not when she's just leaving the hospital."

"If you said them, then they needed to be said. The truth is always best. Breaking an entrenched pattern of behavior is difficult, and maybe it has to begin with brutal honesty. If Alice is determined to take her own life, I know from experience there's very little anyone else can do to stop her. But I don't think she'll try again. If she should, then you need to remember what you said to your daughter. You are not responsible for Alice's happiness, or her life. She is. And she knows how to reach me if she needs to talk. I'll check on her right now."

Charlie had just hung up when Lenora said, "Call for you, Charlie. Line two."

He picked up, apprehensive as hell.

"Charlie?" It was Barney, Charlie's contact in Missing Persons. "Listen, pal, I'm up to my neck in alligators, but I wanted to let you know I located that dude you were looking for."

"Gordon Monroe?" Charlie sat up straighter.

"Yeah. Driving a newer Volvo wagon as a taxi service in and around Melaque. It's a little place southwest of Guadalajara. He's using a set of what are probably stolen license plates, transporting tourists up and down the coast. Nothing we can really charge him with. I've got some photos of him and I'll e-mail them over to you, but he's your man all right."

"How'd you locate him?"

"We're working on finding another guy, who skipped bail on a drug charge, and we figure he's down in that area of Mexico. I gave my contact with the Mexican *federales* your guy's info, along with our other friend's folder. Juan put out the word, and yours turned up before mine did."

"Pretty hard to just disappear."

"Ain't that the truth."

"Is there a phone number, or any way he can be reached?"

"There's a little store where he picks up messages. People who want cab service leave notes for him there. The woman who runs it would probably give him a heads-up, but she doesn't speak any English. Here, you got a pen?"

Barney rhymed off a long string of numbers, and Charlie copied them down. "Thanks, Barney. I owe you."

"Yeah, well, my nephew's lookin' to buy his first place, so I'll send him to you and maybe you can find him a deal."

"Do my best." Was he getting a client in the bargain?

When the ad was done to his satisfaction, Charlie handed it over to Lenora. She'd take care of the details, and it would appear in the paper due out in two days.

He went to his car and dialed Bella on his cell.

"You mind if I drop by for a few minutes?" He didn't want to tell her about her ex over the phone.

"Come ahead. I was about to call you—we really should go over and get going on that house."

"Are you free to do that? Did Kelsey calm down? I'm really sorry."

"After a fashion. She's in her room with her cell phone, probably calling social services as we speak, claiming child abuse."

"Well, you're likely facing jail time, but I've heard the food in the pen isn't that bad anymore. Be there in twenty minutes."

BELLA WAS WAITING for him when he pulled into the driveway. They loaded paint and lumber and other supplies from the garage into the back of the pick-up, and then climbed into the truck.

Charlie asked again, "Are you sure Kelsey's okay? I feel awful that she walked in on us that way."

"Yeah, me, too. She's living in a dream world, though, believing Gordon's going to come back and we'll turn into a happy family. It's not going to help for me to tell her the truth, which is that her father has bailed on all of us and probably won't be in touch anytime soon. If ever."

He started the motor. "Should we be leaving her alone?"

Bella nodded. "She's okay on her own for a few hours. She was sleeping just now when I checked, and she'll feel better if she naps for a while. I left a note for Josh to phone me the minute he gets in."

"I had a call from Barney. He's found your ex." Soon-to-be, at least, so terminology didn't matter. But Charlie would still feel a lot better once that happened. He told her how Barney had located Gordon. "He's using your Volvo as a cab, taking people from one town to the next."

"While I pay the lease. That creep. He's got some nerve. Wouldn't he have to have a special license to run a cab service?"

"Not down there. He probably just had to bribe somebody. Barney said he was using different license plates, probably stolen."

"I'm going to get that car back, Charlie. Even if I have to go down there myself and drive it away. I still have the spare keys. And I'll get divorce papers from Niki's uncle, so I can serve him those, as well."

"Sort of one-stop shopping." Charlie was thinking how great it would be to take off with her, drive down the coast, away from the rain into the sunshine. Stay at motels every night. But there were all sorts of reasons that plan wouldn't work. Such as her kids, his job, Emma. And there was the tiny matter of money.

"There's a phone number at a store where he picks up messages. The lady that runs it doesn't speak English. How's your Spanish?"

"I could probably bungle through, but I don't want him to know I've located him. I want it to be a surprise."

"That's probably a smart move. You going to tell the kids?"

"Yes. They have a right to know."

"If you go, will you take them with?"

"I don't know. I'll have to think about it."

They'd reached the house. It hadn't improved any since the last time they were here.

They got out and unloaded supplies.

Inside, Bella looked around and shook her head. "Do you think there's any hope, Charlie?"

He suspected she wasn't asking about the house at all.

CHAPTER SIXTEEN

CHARLIE DROPPED BELLA OFF at home later that afternoon. He'd wanted to speak to Josh, and when the boy came to the door, Charlie asked if he'd like to have a game of squash.

"Yeah, I'd like that." Josh tried to sound cool, but he couldn't subdue the excitement in his eyes or the huge grin that spread across his face.

"Good," Charlie said. "I don't have my brother's card for Jericho, but I found out there's courts at Shaughnessy Community Center. I can stop in and make a reservation on my way home. Seven tonight okay with you?"

"Yeah, great. See you then."

As she opened tins of tomato soup and slapped together cheese sandwiches to grill for dinner, Bella thought about the change that had taken place in Josh's attitude toward Charlie. He'd earned her son's trust, and she was grateful. The boy needed a strong male presence in his life.

Don't we all, she thought, putting bowls and plates on the counter.

Josh hurried in when she called that dinner was ready. Kelsey was still sleeping—or pretending to—when Bella stuck her head in the bedroom.

Bella hesitated, and then closed the door softly. There was that old adage about sleeping dogs.

She missed Kelsey's suggestions in the kitchen about food. The girl had a natural gift in that area. But most of all, Bella missed their newfound closeness. She thought of the sweet little girl who'd borrowed her shoes for dress up and cried the first day of school; who'd carried a small handbag of Bella's with her all during the first grade, so she'd have something of her mother's with her at all times.

How Bella wished she could find a way to help her accept that Gordon wasn't coming back, to ease the pain that acknowledgment would cause. But Bella knew from her own experience it was a realization Kelsey would have to come to on her own.

Her daughter hadn't made an appearance by the time Charlie came for Josh. Bella cleaned up the remains of the meal, and as she worked, she thought again about Charlie. Workwise, they made a good team. They'd accomplished more today than she'd expected, with him doing the carpentry and her painting walls. It was fun working with him—more fun than it had ever been working with Gordon at the hardware store.

She and Charlie bantered back and forth, and sometimes they talked seriously. They also argued intensely, but there was no animosity between them. She couldn't help but compare Charlie and Gordon; they were the only men she'd spent much time with during her adult years. Charlie had a generosity of spirit she'd never known before.

And now that Charlie had located Gordon, she had to decide what she was going to do about him. Go to Mexico by herself? Take the kids? But before any of those decisions could be made, she had to first tell them where their father was. She wasn't looking forward to it. She was pretty certain Kelsey, for one, would want to head straight to Melaque.

Her daughter came downstairs eventually, obviously motivated by hunger.

"Can I make you a grilled cheese sandwich?" Bella reached for the frying pan, but Kelsey pulled it away from her.

"I can do it myself, thank you."

"Kelsey, rudeness is not an option here. I realize you're upset, but you won't speak to me in that tone."

"Sorry."

It was barely a mumble, but Bella decided to pretend it was a full-scale apology.

"Are you feeling better? Have the cramps eased?"

The girl gave an offhand shrug. "They're not too bad now." She busied herself making a sandwich. "The heating pad helps."

At least this was a neutral subject. At least they were speaking.

Bella said, "I used to get them really bad. Mom would fill a hot-water bottle for me and give me aspirin." Bella made chamomile tea and poured them each a cup.

"Nana said she used to throw up when she got the curse."

"Do girls still call it that?"

Kelsey shrugged. "Sometimes, yeah."

"I wonder if it's inherited, getting bad cramps?" Bella was clutching at straws to keep the conversation going.

Kelsey brought her sandwich to the table and sat down. "Maybe it comes from Daddy's side, too. Not that there's anybody I could ask."

Bella nodded. "I know. It's hard not having lots of relatives. I used to wish I was part of Niki's family, with all those aunts and uncles and cousins."

"Yeah, Auntie Niki's really lucky. Except I don't like her uncle Vinnie—he always pinches my cheeks."

"I guess there's a downside to it. Niki had a

really mean grandma, I know that. Ruthie, her name was. She was Niki's father's mother. She used to make Niki and me clean her house for her while she smoked and drank whiskey and watched game shows on TV. She'd try and hit us with the broom handle if we didn't get things clean enough."

"No way." Kelsey's blue eyes were wide. "You never told me that before. She'd actually hit you?"

"Yup, she'd try. But we knew how to stay out of her reach. We were faster than she was."

"Nana would never hit me." Kelsey took small, dainty bites of her sandwich.

"I should hope not. Your nana dotes on you and Josh." Kelsey ate just the way Mae did, Bella realized, taking those tiny bites, chewing slowly. And she had Mae's amazing blue eyes.

"What's the score with her and Grandpa? How come they hate each other so much?"

"I'm not exactly sure, honey." Bella remembered the conversation with her mother. "I do know that at first they cared for each other, but I don't know exactly what happened to change that."

"But you and Daddy don't hate each other, right?"

"No, Kelsey. We certainly don't." Bella hated getting back to this subject, though.

"So maybe you'll get back together. Right?"

"Kelsey. Sweetheart. I don't think that's likely. I don't want you to expect that to happen."

Without another word, Kelsey got up, put her plate in the dishwasher and headed back upstairs.

Bella sighed, poured another cup of tea and took it into the living room. At least for a little while there'd been an open window for her and her daughter. All she could hope was that it would open again, and soon.

Josh came home shortly afterward, flushed and pleased with himself, giving Bella a play-by-play account of the games he and Charlie had had. She listened, delighted her son had enjoyed himself.

"I can take him, Mom, I know I can. I just need a little more practice."

"In your dreams." Kelsey had come downstairs and plopped into an armchair. She obviously knew where Josh had been, because she said in a scathing tone, "Don't be such a dweeb, Josh. It's Mother he likes, not you."

Bella braced herself, expecting Kelsey to blurt out next that she'd seen them kissing. But she didn't. She did shoot Bella a knowing glance.

Josh, oblivious to undercurrents, just shrugged. "So what's wrong with that? Can't he like all of us? He's going to take me out for a few driving lessons if Mom says it's okay."

Kelsey rolled her eyes. "You are *so* pathetic." She got up and headed for the stairs again.

"Kelsey, wait a moment, please, I need to talk to you both." Bella took a deep breath. "I've found out where your father is." She related everything Charlie had told her.

Kelsey said in an eager voice, "So when can we go and see him?"

Josh sent his sister a disbelieving look, but to his credit, didn't say anything.

Bella said, "I don't know, Kelse. I have to think about this and figure out what's best to do." Maybe it would help Kelsey to see her father, and ask him the questions she needed answers for.

"Mother." Her voice held total disdain. "Get a grip. We know where Daddy is now, so why not just go down there and visit him? He's our father— he must miss us and he'll be glad if we come, right?"

Josh shot a look at Bella that said, *Do you believe this?*

And that's when she realized how much he'd matured in the past several months, and how much he really understood. Her son was growing up fast. He recognized that Gordon had deserted them, and he was doing his best to move on, but poor Kelsey clung stubbornly to her dreams.

Bella swallowed the lump in her throat. She said, "I'll decide in the next few days what's best, and I promise I'll tell you as soon as I make up my mind."

"That's just *pitiful*. I have a right to see my daddy." Kelsey flounced back up the stairs.

"She just doesn't get it," Josh said in a disgusted voice. "I've tried to tell her, but she won't listen. He walked out on us, he's never bothered to phone or write, and he doesn't give a damn. But she won't admit it. She was always his precious pet, so no wonder she can't accept he doesn't want anything to do with us anymore."

Bella wanted so much to deny it, but Gordon's actions were indefensible. "I'm sure he loves you and Kelsey, Josh." It was weak, but what else could she say?

"Yeah, right." He got up and went into the kitchen. Bella followed. "He left you with all the bills, right? And he took the good car." Josh pulled out the garbage from under the sink and, without Bella having to remind him, tied the bag and carried it outside.

When he came back in, he switched subjects so quickly that it took Bella off guard. "So where's Grandpa these days? How come he's not coming over? He promised he'd take me out for driving lessons, too."

Would it never end? Bella drew a deep breath.

"I told him and your nana that they weren't welcome around here until they learned to put their differences aside and act like responsible adults."

Josh's eyes widened. "You told them not to come around? Geez, Mom. Why'd you have to go and do a thing like that?"

"Because we have enough problems around here without listening to them hashing over past grievances. They're old enough to know better."

"Well, excellent." Josh's voice dripped with disgust. "Way to go, Mom. Just cut us off from the entire world, why don't you? If it wasn't for Charlie, I'd never learn how to drive. You are going to let him teach me, aren't you?"

"I'll discuss it with him." It wasn't good for Josh to think he'd bullied her into the decision.

He gave her a critical look and stomped off to his room, leaving Bella wondering if it wouldn't be best to just put both her kids up for adoption and be done with it. Obviously, her parenting skills were somewhere below zero.

SHE WAS CONSIDERING a hot bath and an early night when the doorbell rang. Her heart lifted when she saw it was Charlie.

"I dropped by the office on my way home and picked up the proofs for the ad. I'd like you to see them before they're published."

"C'mon in. You don't need an excuse to come by, you know."

He leaned forward to kiss her, then thought better of it. "Kids around?"

"Upstairs. Both pissed off with me, big time. Different reasons, same result."

"Sorry. It's never easy, is it?" He took off his coat and she hung it up. It was raining again, and Bella thought of Mexico, and Gordon basking in the sun. Here she was in the cold and wet, with Kelsey and Josh hating her. Would there ever come a time when she and her kids were at peace? It wore her down, constantly being the bad guy in their lives.

She longed to fling herself into Charlie's arms and be comforted, but if Kelsey walked in on another scenario like that, there'd be more hell to pay. So instead Bella led the way into the kitchen, consoling herself a little by taking Charlie's hand.

His big fingers closed tight around hers.

"Tea? I was having some myself."

"Please." He gave her hand an extra squeeze and released it to open a folder. He spread several sheets out on the island. "What d'ya think of these?"

She picked one up and her spirits lifted. "That's my house? Wow, it looks fabulous. You've done a great job on these, Charlie."

"There'll be an open house on Saturday, and I'm hoping we have decent offers by that evening."

"Wouldn't that be something? Then I can start looking around for somewhere to move to."

"As for finding something to rent, I brought

the listings we have for rental properties. They're not great, but maybe there's something here that would suit you."

Bella studied them. The ones she might be able to afford were anything but appealing. In fact, they were downright depressing. She held them out and wrinkled her nose.

"Yuck. They look pretty dismal."

Charlie studied them. "Yeah, I know. But remember, we can upgrade with paint and elbow grease."

"I need to also remember that beggars can't be choosers."

"You'll come out of this fine." He put a hand on her arm. "I'm going to get the best deal for you I can possibly arrange, Bella."

He sounded so serious. She smiled at him, puzzled. "Of course you are. I've never doubted that for a moment."

"Just so you know."

"I'm glad I won't have to be here for the open house. I couldn't live through another session like that one with the Schulmans."

He seemed about to say something, but when she raised a quizzical eyebrow, he obviously changed his mind.

She turned her attention back to the rental houses. "Maybe I should go and have a look at some of these. Just in case."

"We can do that anytime you want."

He left soon afterward, and this time he did kiss her, deeply and hungrily. When the door closed behind him, Bella leaned against it, trembling with need. It was so delicious to feel passionate, to know Charlie felt exactly the same. It was so frustrating not to be able to take it to its logical conclusion.

HE SHOULD HAVE TOLD HER the truth about the Schulmans. The opportunity was right there, and he'd blown it. The truth was, he was ashamed of Rick, ashamed to admit that his own brother could be so dishonest. Charlie wanted Bella to trust him. Because of the listing, he assured himself.

And also, he reasoned, if he'd told her, she'd have guessed immediately that the story, including certain embarrassing details, must have gone the rounds at the office. She'd be humiliated and embarrassed.

He didn't want that; she had enough to contend with. He'd done the best thing, keeping quiet.

Weird how sometimes the best thing made you feel so damn lousy.

SATURDAY MORNING, Bella was up at dawn, nervously cleaning every last corner she'd missed the evening before. She wanted everything perfect for the open house.

She got Josh and Kelsey up, did a final inspection on their rooms and all the bathrooms, and hurried them out the door. The open house started at ten and ended at three, but rather than have breakfast and then have to clean the kitchen all over again, she took them to a pancake house, screw the expense.

Niki had invited them all over for the day, and Josh and Kelsey were also spending the night there. They were excited because Tom was taking them to a motorcycle rally that afternoon. Kelsey still wasn't saying much beyond the basic bare necessities to Bella, but at least she was polite.

Everyone enjoyed breakfast. Bella was touched when both Josh and Kelsey thanked her for taking them.

Soon after they arrived at Niki and Tom's, Tom left with the teens in tow, and Niki poured coffee for Bella and herself. They settled into the big overstuffed chairs in her living room.

"I'm grateful for this, Niki, but how come you're not at the salon today?"

"I've been spotting some, and the doctor said to take it easy, so I hired this gal to run the place. She calls herself, get this, Galatea. She's six feet tall and mega scary. I'm pretty sure she's the result of a sex change, but she runs the joint like clockwork. Susie hasn't been late once since Galatea arrived on the scene."

Bella sent up a silent, fervent prayer that Niki and the baby would be fine. "You feeling okay, apart from spotting?"

"Sick as a dog every morning. I love it." Niki burrowed deeper into the cushions. "I've waited half my life for morning sickness and intend to enjoy every heave. So now dish me all the good stuff about you and Charlie boy."

So for the next quarter hour, Bella did. It was exhilarating to be able to talk about him freely, to admit the way she felt—the way he made her feel. It took her mind off money, bills, the problems with her parents, the kids, and whether or not the house was going to sell.

And she realized it also took Niki's mind off the possibility of losing her precious baby. When Bella finally ran out of steam, her friend said, "So what are you going to do about old scumbag?"

"I'm not sure yet." Bella had told her about Charlie locating Gordon.

"You're going down there to get the car back, right?"

"I need to wait until the house sells. There's no way I can spare any money at all until that happens."

"Well, when you do decide to go, invite Charlie along, why don't you? Tom and I'll keep Josh and Kelsey. We'd love to have them here for a while. It looks like I'll be working less, so I'd enjoy the company."

"Thanks. You're the best friend a mother could have. But if I took off with Charlie to Mexico and left Kelsey behind, God only knows what she'd do."

Bella explained about Kelsey seeing her and Charlie kissing. "She's got it in her head that Gordon is the victim in all this, and that he's just waiting anxiously for her to visit him. The only obstacle is me."

Niki shook her head. "Poor little miss. She's in for some big, hard awakenings."

"I know, and it makes me sad. She's my little girl. I hate to see her get hurt."

"I'll see if she'll open up to me and maybe talk out some of her feelings. We've always had a connection, Kelsey and I."

"She adores you. And she needs somebody besides Mae or me to talk to." Bella grinned. "Remember how we went through that time when we figured our mothers were mentally challenged? Well, that's what's going on with her and me."

"She's thirteen. It's her job to be obnoxious."

"There's lots of times lately when I feel sorry for what I put Mae through."

"Have you told her that?"

"No. I haven't spoken to her since the day I told her to try and get along with Oscar."

"You were right doing that. The kids don't need the aggravation."

"Yeah, but I may never see Mom or Oscar again."

"You will, take my word for it. Kelsey and Josh are like magnets for them, and they'll come around."

"Thanks, Little Miss Sunshine. And thanks, as well, for keeping my kids tonight." Bella felt her cheeks get warm. "I'm going to invite Charlie over."

It wasn't a holiday in Mexico, but to Bella it felt just as good.

Niki threw up both thumbs in a victory sign. "*Yes*. I've got some of that new warming lotion— you want to borrow it? Or sexy underwear, I've got tons of that. Bubble bath, get him in a bubble bath. Tom loves it when I bathe him."

Bella laughed. "I'll just go with the basics this time, and then when the novelty starts to wear off I'll try kinky. But thanks, anyway."

"Kinky? Me? Girl, you need a course in intercourse."

They spent the rest of the afternoon laughing, and Bella barely had time to wonder how the open house was going.

Charlie wasn't there when Bella returned home late that afternoon, and she was a little disappointed. The house looked the same as when she'd left it, but there was an eerie sense that strangers had been there. She walked through, aware of how beautiful and clean it looked. It was sad that, now it was finally finished, she wouldn't be around to enjoy it. Surely someone would want to buy it?

And someone did. The excitement in Charlie's voice gave him away when he called an hour later.

CHAPTER SEVENTEEN

"CAN I COME OVER, Bella? I have several offers to present to you."

"Come. Hurry." Hope and anticipation made her heart hammer.

He walked in twenty minutes later, and Bella hurled herself into his arms. He tasted of coffee and cool air, and he smelled of someone else's cigarette smoke and his own special soap.

The kiss ended, and he said, "Where are the kids?"

She laughed. "I'm going to make a recording of you asking that question. They're staying with Niki and Tom tonight. Niki said to tell you it's her gift to us, and that there'll be strings attached."

"I can live with that." He laughed, too, pulling her close for another, longer kiss. They were both vibrating when it ended.

Bella said, "Maybe we should go upstairs for a while?"

Charlie shook his head. "After I tell you about

these offers. I can't concentrate properly until then."

"Okay, then make it fast. We're wasting precious time here."

Charlie kissed her again and then pulled a sheaf of paper out of his briefcase. "We have three solid offers."

Bella squealed and jumped up and down. "Three? Oh, my God, three."

"Come and sit down and I'll explain them." With his arm around her shoulders, he led the way into the living room and sat beside her.

"The first is for this amount." He handed Bella the signed paper, pointing out the figure with his forefinger.

Bella read it and felt a little disappointed. The offer was lower than she'd hoped for, and with real-estate commission, it wouldn't quite cover her debts.

Charlie had been watching her face, and he knew what she was thinking. "It's a good offer, there's no subject clause, so no problems that way. It also gives you two months to move, which is a good thing."

"Particularly when I have nowhere to move to," she agreed, trying to quell her disappointment.

He handed over the second. "This one's substantially higher, but there's a subject. The buyer needs to sell his houseboat before he can come up with the down payment. Its high-end, three bed-rooms, parked down at Granville Island. He asked if you'd be interested in taking it and reducing the price on this house. It's an option, because it would give you a place to live, but I told him I thought you'd want the money instead."

"You thought right." Bella was feeling anxious. "I really need cash to get myself out of this finan-cial hole." What if none of these offers worked? She'd had no idea this could be so complicated. What if she was right back at the beginning again, without a sale?

Charlie handed her the third sheet, and Bella's heart leaped when she saw the figure. It was far beyond what she'd hoped for, substantially higher even than the astronomical asking price Charlie had established. Even with the commission, she'd have enough to pay everything off. She'd end up with a small nest egg at the end.

"Charlie. Oh, Charlie, this is fabulous." Too thrilled to stay sitting, she jumped up and did a couple twirls.

He watched her, smiling. "Before you get too carried away, let me explain. This offer came in from clients of Janice Feldergast. It's high because it includes furniture, and there's another catch. These people are moving here from Europe and want somewhere right away. The biggest draw-back is that you'd have to be out in seven days. But the offer's clean—no subjects, no conditions. And you'd get your money fast."

"Seven days?" Bella gasped and plopped back in her seat. "One week, to pack everything and get out?"

Just in this one room, even if the furniture stayed, there was a monumental amount that would need to be packed. She couldn't afford a moving company, either.

Feeling overwhelmed, she imagined all their belongings in all the other rooms. Could she do it in seven days? It seemed impossible. And what would she do for furniture, even if she managed to find somewhere else to live in that short a time? All of a sudden, the walls seemed to be closing in on her.

"You have until tomorrow morning to respond to the other two, but Janice's offer is only open until seven tonight. These people are in a hurry. But give yourself at least that much time to think about it, why don't you?"

Bella slumped against the sofa back, elation tempered by reality.

"To misquote Mae, every silver lining has a cloud," she said. "But I don't think I have much choice, Charlie. The bottom line for me is money, and the third offer is substantially higher than the others. I'm going to have to take it. Somehow, I'll have to meet the conditions."

Charlie was watching her, his face somber. "There's another thing, Bella. Because this is Janice's offer, the split we agreed on with the commission will be less for each of us. She's going to expect her full share."

Bella nodded. "But even so, this offer's going to net me a lot more cash than either of the others, right?"

Charlie nodded in turn.

"Then call Janice right now and tell her I accept the offer."

"You sure you don't want to think it over?"

"I'm sure. Let's just do it."

"Okay. I'll need your signature on the contract. We'll drive it over to the office and drop it off. Janice insists she needs it signed, sealed and delivered by seven this evening."

It was scary, now that the moment had arrived. "And then we'll come back here and celebrate, right, Charlie?"

"Absolutely. I'll bring the champagne. All you need to do is take your clothes off the moment we get in the door."

"Done deal."

AN HOUR AND TWENTY minutes later, they were in bed in the spare room. Their champagne glasses sat on the bedside table, only half-consumed.

This time, their lovemaking was both simpler

and more complex. There was a familiarity with one another's bodies, and a more profound connection. There was also a sense of play that delighted and excited Bella.

"I love being here with you like this." Charlie was touching her, fingers and palms skimming throat and breasts and belly, memorizing her. "I look at you when we're working at that house, and you make me so hot I just want to lay you down on the floor and get you naked."

Bella shuddered. "Not on those floors." She was having trouble talking. "Do that more, okay?"

"This?" He stroked the hollow of her hipbone, a slow and sensuous movement.

"I didn't know how good that could feel. Who knew hipbones were sexy?"

"Me. I knew you were sexy everywhere, even when you threw that cup at me."

"Did I ever apologize for that? Ohh, that's wonderful. Don't stop."

An instant later, it felt even better, because he replaced fingers with lips and gentle nips of teeth.

"Is this better—or this?"

She caught her breath. "You sound like my optometrist. Can you see this better, or this?"

Charlie raised his head and grinned up at her. "Aha, your fantasies are surfacing."

She giggled, a touch hysterically. "Dream on. He's short and round and bald. Don't talk, okay?"

"No accounting for taste. Umm, you taste good."

And then *she* couldn't talk, because his mouth and tongue had moved to yet another zone. And this one sent her up and over, urgent and ecstatic.

THE PHONE HAD RUNG several times while they were making love, and they'd ignored it.

Bella finally got around to retrieving her messages when they came downstairs much later to scramble eggs and make toast. Lovemaking was hungry work. Charlie looked rumpled and sexy, chest bare, denim pants low on his hips.

Bella had pulled on her old fuzzy robe, thinking that Niki would expire if she saw it. And her friend was right—Bella really was going to have to find something sexier. When the sale went through, she'd buy herself a see-through black something or other and drive Charlie wild. She'd go to the expert and ask Niki's advice.

"It's Janice. She wants to talk to me," Bella said, listening to the woman's second voice mail. "She doesn't say why."

"Better call her," he advised with a glance at the clock. "It's just after ten—that's not late. Just in case there's something they need clarified. I'll do the eggs while you phone."

Bella dialed the number Janice had left.

"Bella," the other woman said, when the call

connected. "Just wanted to tell you I'm delighted you accepted my client's offer. I have a list of the furniture they'd like and I wanted to run it by you. It's basically just all the appliances, a couple beds, dressers, the dining-room stuff, and the couches and side tables from the living room. Oh, and the stools in the kitchen."

"So what don't they want?" Bella knew she sounded a little acerbic. "Because that list includes most of my stuff."

"I guess it does. Never mind, think of the lovely money." Janice laughed. "And they adored the house, never even asked about under-floor heating or water purifiers. Didn't mention nitrites once."

Bella was confused for a moment. Then she remembered. "Oh, so Charlie told you about the Schulmans?"

"Actually, it was Rick who told me. He was pretty pumped at winning the pool."

"The pool?" Bella was beginning to think Janice had been drinking.

"Oh, didn't Charlie say?" A chirpy giggle followed. "All the guys in the office had a pile of money hanging on Charlie not getting the listing on your place, after they had tried and struck out. But Rick had faith, and he was the one who called in the Schulmans. Oops, me and my big mouth, that probably wasn't something you needed to know. Sorry. And I hear Marlena was a proper pain in the butt." Janice giggled. "She's so dramatic, isn't she? That's actors for you. But all's well that ends well. Now you have a wonderful sale out of the whole deal." Her voice became snide and knowing. "I hope you and Charlie are celebrating in a fitting manner."

Bella managed to say goodbye before she hung up. She was shaking.

"What was Janice on about?" Charlie set a plate of scrambled eggs and buttered toast in front of her. "Here, eat up. Gotta keep up your strength! I plan to drag you back up those stairs the moment you're fed, woman."

Bella sat down, because her knees weren't too steady.

"Charlie."

His mouth was full. He raised his eyebrows, and when he saw her expression, he swallowed. Hard.

"What? What's wrong? Did the deal go south?"

"She said there was a bet, Charlie. At the office." Bella's throat was so dry she had to stop and take a sip of tea. "A bet that you wouldn't get me to agree to listing the house."

Charlie didn't move. She knew by the stricken look on his face that it was true.

Bella felt sick. "And...and she said it was Rick that set up the thing with the Schulmans? They're actors, apparently. That was so I'd get discouraged and give you the listing, right?" She cleared her throat and steadied her hands by putting them palm down on the table.

"Charlie?" She heard the pleading note in her voice. She wanted him to deny it all. She wanted that more than she'd wanted anything in a long time, far more than the sale, or the money, or her parents finding a way to get along, or her kids forgiving her for not being a perfect mother.

"Charlie?" It sounded like a prayer.

He blew out a breath and didn't meet her eyes. "Yeah. Yeah, it's all true. I knew about the bet, but I didn't know about the Schulmans until the other day."

The extent of his duplicity was only beginning to dawn on her. "But…but you didn't tell me."

"No. And I should have." He got up and came around the table, put his hands on her shoulders. "I'm so sorry, Bella."

She shot to her feet, wrenching away from him. "You should have told me. If I'd known they were a setup, I might not have been so quick to… I might have…" She choked as the knowing tone in Janice's voice came back to her. "They all know you're sleeping with me, too, don't they? What a joke, huh? They all think that's how you got me to sign the agreement for sale."

"Bella." Charlie tried to take her in his arms, but she moved back.

He said, "What they think has nothing to do with us. They'll think whatever they want. Don't do this, sweetheart. Let me explain."

"Okay, explain." Her throat was raw. Maybe she was getting the flu? "Is that why you slept with me, Charlie? That's why, isn't it? To get the listing. You wanted to win the bet."

"No." It came out too loud. "Don't be ridiculous. Stop right there and listen to me, okay? In the beginning, yeah, I wasn't entirely honest with you. I wanted the listing, of course I did. But I didn't know you then, not really. It was a challenge, a chance to prove to Rick that I wasn't dead weight at the agency."

"You knew I was desperate. You figured I was pathetic. A good screw and I'd come around— that's what every deserted woman needs, right?"

"Is that what you think of me?" He was angry now, as angry as she was. His eyes narrowed, his voice dropped. "I'm no saint, but I sure as hell would never use a woman to get a listing."

"You'd let your brother use the Schulmans, though."

"I didn't even know Rick knew them. I didn't know anything about that until it was over, Bella, I swear."

"But you knew about the pool. You knew there were bets at the office."

"Yeah. I did know about that." He looked at her

for a long moment. "This isn't getting us anywhere. I think I should go now, and we can talk
when we've both cooled down."

"I think that's probably best." She had so
wanted him to stay. She'd been dreaming of wak-
ing up beside him in the morning, the first chance
they'd had to spend a night together.

He took the stairs two at a time, and came down
with his socks and his shirt on. He pulled on his
shoes and got his coat out of the hall closet.

He was standing by the door when he said, "Do
you want to back out of the sale?"

"No." She'd considered it while he was upstairs.
She hated the thought of having anything more to
do with Janice Feldergast. But canceling the sale
would really be cutting off her nose to spite her
face, in Mae's parlance.

"Okay. I'll call you in the morning and we'll
talk. This isn't over, Bella."

The door closed softly behind him, and it felt
to Bella like abandonment, worse than any she'd
ever endured.

THAT NIGHT WAS ENDLESS. She went over and over
her time with Charlie, trying to find danger signs
she should have heeded. But hell, she'd gone over
and over the years she'd spent with Gordon, and
even there she couldn't see the forest for the trees.

Even the harmonica didn't help. She tried, but it

was impossible to blow and cry at the same time. Totally spent, Bella finally fell asleep at quarter to six, and when the phone rang at nine-forty-five it yanked her from a confusing dream about attics she was trying to clear out, that just kept filling up again.

"The kids are there, right?" It was Niki, and she sounded frantic. "Please tell me Josh and Kelsey are there, Bella."

"Here?" Bella cleared her croaky throat and tried to get her bearings. "I don't know. Did you drop them off already? I didn't hear them. Sorry, I was asleep."

"No, we didn't drop them off. Tom and I just got up and realized they're gone. They're not here. Go and see if they're there, Bella, please. Hurry, okay?"

Taking the phone with her, Bella got out of bed and trotted down the hall. But her children's rooms were still pristine, just the way they'd been yesterday morning. She went downstairs. The house was clean—and empty.

Her heart was thumping, and adrenaline made her jumpy. "They're not here either, Niki. Maybe they took a bus. Maybe they're on their way."

"But why would they leave like this, without a word? We had a great time last night, we watched videos till late, we had popcorn, we were all going out to Chinatown for dim sum this morning. It doesn't make sense they'd just up and leave."

It didn't to Bella, either. She was starting to get scared. "Did they leave a note?"

"Nope. Nothing. Tom went in to wake them up and they were gone. Their backpacks are missing, and their coats. The beds are made—I can't tell if they slept in them or not." Niki's voice trembled. "I'm going a little nuts here, Bella. How the hell could we lose your kids?"

Bella subdued her own alarm bells long enough to be rational with Niki. "Calm down, okay? They're not babies, and nobody would abduct both of them." But even as Bella said it, fear made her shiver. What if some maniac…?

"Bella, is Charlie there?"

"No. We had a fight last night, and he didn't stay."

"Well, fight or not, get hold of him. He was a cop, and he'll know what to do."

"Look, Niki, Kelsey has her cell phone. Maybe she's trying to call me. I'll hang up, and the moment I hear from them, I'll let you know."

Bella raced upstairs and pulled on jeans and a shirt, keeping the phone within arm's reach, willing it to ring. When it finally did, she pounced on it and shrieked, "Kelsey? Where the *hell* are you?"

After a shocked instant, Charlie said, "It's me, Bella. What's going on over there?"

She was too rattled to do anything but tell him. She kept gulping, as if she couldn't get enough air.

He was silent for a moment. Then he said, "Have you called your mother? They might be there."

Relief spilled through Bella. Of course that's where they'd gone. She said a quick goodbye and hung up, then dialed Mae's number.

"Mom? Are the kids with you?"

"No, of course they're not." Mae's tone was as aggrieved as ever. "Why would they be? If you remember, you're the one who forbade me to see my own grandchildren. And I'm not getting any younger, Annabella, I hope you keep that in mind."

Bella was hyperventilating, trying to stave off a panic attack. There was one other option. "Mom, do you happen to have Oscar's phone number?"

After a moment of silence, Mae said, "Why on earth would *I* have such a thing? Unlike you, I have no desire to ever set eyes on that man again—"

Bella, on the verge of hysteria, shouted at her. "Mom, *shut up* and listen to me for once. Josh and Kelsey stayed with Niki and Tom last night. They were gone when Niki got up this morning. She doesn't know if they slept there, where they are or why they'd disappear this way. They didn't leave a note or anything. I need to find them, fast. If they're with Oscar, I need to know." And she waited for the hysterics on the other end to begin.

Instead, Mae said in a controlled voice, "Okay. You stay right there, Annabella, in case they phone home. Call the police. I'll get a cab, go over to Oscar's and find out if he's seen them. I'll call you from there."

Stunned, Bella hung up, just in time to answer the doorbell and let Charlie in.

He looked rumpled. He hadn't shaved. He had the same bags under his eyes that she had. "No kids yet?"

She tried to answer and couldn't because her throat closed up. She just shook her head and wrapped her arms around her breasts.

Without a single word, he enfolded her in his arms. Suddenly the issues that had seemed so important last night were no longer huge. Bella rested against his chest, breathing in his scent, comforted because she was no longer alone.

She whispered, "What am I going to do, Charlie?"

"I'll call Barney, and he'll put the word out to the guys on the street to watch for them. Then we'll phone Greyhound, see if they might have taken a bus. There are rules about selling tickets to underage kids, but Josh is one smart guy. If he wanted to get around rules, he'd probably find a way."

"Kelsey has her cell phone. I keep praying she'll call."

"Okay, I'll use mine so your line is open." He pulled it out and began dialing as Bella's phone rang.

She snatched it up. It was Niki.

"Bella, we just found a note. It was under Tom's shaving kit in the bathroom. Here, I'll read it." She had to clear her throat twice, and when she finally got her voice working, it warbled up and down the scale.

Dear Niki and Tom, K and I have gone to find our dad. We took some money from the jar in your cupboard—I promise we'll pay it back. Please call Mom and let her know so she won't worry too much. We'll phone when we get there. Sorry about the money. K was going to go by herself, the idiot, and I couldn't let her. Josh.

"How—how much money did they take?"

"It was my tip jar. Probably around six hundred. Not that I care, just that it might help to know they aren't going to starve."

There was a knock on the door. Bella answered it, phone still in hand.

"Niki, my mom and dad are here. I'll call you the minute we know anything more."

"What can we do?" Mae bustled in and Oscar followed. Bella could see his psychedelic car, parked crossways in the drive.

"Oscar gave me a ride. He hasn't seen them, either," Mae confirmed. As she took her coat off, she said, "Have you heard anything?"

"Yes, Niki found a note." Bella recited it from memory. Josh's words were burned on her brain.

Charlie listened and then said, "They must have taken the bus, then, probably first to Seattle. I'd be surprised if they make it across the border—they'll need photo ID there. Do they have passports, Bella?"

"No." She shook her head. "They have their birth certificates, though. On those laminated cards. With their pictures." She was breathing in short little gasps.

"Even with those, they'd never manage to get on a plane—security's too tight for that," Charlie stated. "Greyhound's checking, but didn't think there were any unaccompanied teens on the bus this morning. Now they have to locate the ticket agent who was on duty last night."

Bella said, "They wouldn't hitchhike, would they?" Her voice broke.

"Josh has way too much sense for that." Oscar put an arm around her. "Charlie, it's good that you're here." He held out his other hand and Charlie shook it.

Bella was trying to figure out what to do next. She could only think of one thing. "I'm phoning Gordon. If there's the slightest possibility they make it to Mexico, he has to watch out for them." She found the scrap of paper where she'd written down the number Charlie had given her.

It took several tries before she got through, and her Spanish was woefully rusty. She was as tense as a drum by the time the call ended. "I couldn't remember the word for husband," she confessed. "Mental block. But I think I got the message across for Gordon to call here, that it was an emergency."

"I'm making coffee." Mae headed for the kitchen.

They were all drinking it by the time the next call came.

Bella pounced on the phone. The man on the line was soft-spoken and very polite. He had Bella identify herself before he'd say why he'd called.

When she had, he said, "Ma'am, my name is Scott Gillis. I'm a U.S. security officer at Blaine, Washington. We have two youngsters here who were on a Greyhound bus—Josh and Kelsey Monroe? We've detained them until you can confirm they're traveling with your consent."

"They're not, I mean, yes, they're mine," Bella babbled. "And they ran away—I'm half out of my mind worrying about them. Please, please, keep them there until I can come for them. Don't let them out of your sight for a moment."

"Will do, ma'am. They'll be here with us until you get here. Would you like to speak to them?"

"Oh, God, yes. Please."

"They're at the U.S. border," Bella told the others before Josh came on the line. Oscar cheered, and Mae joined in. Charlie smiled at Bella.

"Hello, Mom?" Josh sounded subdued.

"Oh, Josh." Bella was crying now. "Honey, I'm so glad you're okay. What were you thinking, running away like this? I was terrified. Everyone is. Is Kelsey okay?"

"Yeah, she's fine." His voice dropped to a disgusted whisper. "Apart from being a brainless nerd. I told her this would never work, but she's such a baby. She was going to run away by herself, without any money or anything, and I couldn't let her do that. Tell Aunt Niki I've still got most of her money, and I'm really sorry for taking it."

"Okay. Okay, we'll talk about that later." Bella was already thinking of suitable consequences for that little performance. "We'll be there as soon as we can to bring you home."

"Hurry, okay, Mom?" Bella could hardly hear him when he added in a desperate whisper, "These guys have *guns*."

The next half hour was chaotic. Everyone wanted to come along to collect Josh and Kelsey, but no one's vehicle was big enough. Charlie finally suggested he and Bella take his truck, and Oscar and Mae drive down in Bella's car. That would leave room for the kids on the way home.

Bella braced herself for the argument her parents would invariably get into over that arrangement, but to her amazement, all they hassled over was who would drive. Considering that Mae hadn't, to Bella's knowledge, driven so much as a bicycle for as long as she could remember, and had no driver's license, Oscar easily won.

They were about to leave when the phone rang again.

"I have a collect call for Bella Monroe from Gordon Monroe. Will you accept the charges?"

She ought to have guessed he'd call collect. Bella couldn't decide whether to laugh or cry—or refuse the charges.

"Yeah, I'll accept."

"Bella?"

It was a shock to hear Gordon's voice. She'd rehearsed during many long nights the scathing things she'd say when she spoke to him again, but she just couldn't muster up the energy for righteous rage now. She was far too grateful to have her kids safe, too drained by the emotional few hours she'd just spent.

Quietly, she explained to Gordon that Josh and Kelsey had run away to find him. She added that they'd been picked up at the border.

He said, "They're both okay?"

"They're fine. I'm going to get them now." She could hear voices in the background, bursts of rapid Spanish, laughter. He was obviously in a public place, probably the store.

"You know, Kelsey actually believes you still care about her," she couldn't help but say.

"Of course I care—she's my kid. They're both my kids," he sputtered.

"Yeah? Pretty hard to believe you have any feelings for them when you walked out like you did and haven't even contacted them once," Bella said.

She was getting some indignation back now, and it felt good. "You left us penniless, Gordon. You even took the Volvo, knowing I'd have to pay the lease. And you left me with a mountain of other bills. What the heck did you do with all our money?" It was the question that had haunted her.

"Mining stock." He sighed. "I traded online and took risks on some mining stock."

"Good God!" She wanted to ask him what kind of irresponsible move that was, but instead said, "Why didn't you just tell me?"

"Because you wouldn't have understood, Bella. It's always been your way or the highway. You never really listened to me, you just reacted and exploded. I couldn't face another big fight with you."

Was that really how she'd been? That was obviously how he perceived her. She needed to think about it, and if it was true, make some serious changes.

"I want the Volvo back, Gordon. I need you to return it—I'm broke." There was also the matter of the divorce papers, but one thing at a time. "I had to sell the house, and I have to be out in a week." The reality of that hadn't quite hit her, not with all that was happening this morning. "The least you could do is either pay the lease on the car or give it back, so I can turn it in."

"Okay. I'll bring it back."

For a moment, she didn't think she'd heard him properly. "Bring it? Did you say you'd bring it?"

"I want to see the kids. I do have a right to see my kids, Bella."

What was it Mae said all the time? *Better late than never.* And the other one—*I'll believe that when it happens.* Bella wanted to lay both of them on this weak man who had been her husband.

Instead, she had sense enough to just say good-bye.

CHAPTER EIGHTEEN

IN THE TRUCK on the way to Blaine, Charlie did most of the talking.

Bella practiced keeping quiet, in case Gordon had a point. Maybe she didn't listen enough?

Charlie was threading his way through Vancouver traffic, laying out his case on the fight they'd had. "Like I told you, in the beginning I just saw it as a challenge, getting you to list with me, Bella."

The southbound traffic on Oak Street was hellish, stop and start. One thing about being in the truck, Bella thought. Neither of them could walk out. Maybe they ought to schedule all their fights in a moving vehicle.

Charlie stopped at yet another light and turned toward her.

"From the minute you beaned me with that cup, I thought you were sexy and funny and stubborn as hell. I wanted the listing—it was a challenge because you were so bullheaded. Sure, I had fantasies about taking you to bed—I'm a red-blooded male. I admit it. Then I got to know you and the kids a little more, and I still wanted to get you in bed, but the listing wasn't as important. I got to know you, Bella. I liked you. Things changed."

So maybe she wasn't such a horrible woman, after all.

The light changed. They were moving again. Charlie kept up his monologue. It was sort of restful, not having to answer every issue. This listening thing was okay; she could do this.

"Rick's my brother, but he and I aren't alike in lots of ways. He wants the big car, executive home, Italian suits. I'm just not wired that way. I never will be, no matter how many houses I sell."

Had she ever seen him in anything but jeans? Nope. She didn't need to. She liked him in jeans. She liked him even better out of them.

A woman in a red Audi pulled past them and gave Charlie the finger. He didn't even see her. Bella resisted the impulse to return the gesture. Maybe she'd changed into a kinder, gentler person? Maybe some of her rough edges finally had been worn down.

He was saying, "Honest to God, I was furious when I found out about the Schulman thing, Bella. I didn't have a clue Rick was pulling that, and I'd never seen those people before. I can see how it must look to you, as if I used every trick in the book to get you to list, but I didn't. I honestly just wanted the best for you. I really care about you,

Bella. I care about Kelsey and Josh, as well. I don't have the best track record when it comes to being a father, but I learn from my mistakes. Did I tell you Emma's gotten some counseling? She's dating somebody and she's lost ten pounds. She's always been self-conscious about her weight. I haven't met the guy yet. He'd better be good enough for her."

They were on the highway now, and he pulled into the other lane and passed a semi. When they were back in the right lane, he said, with a catch in his throat, "Bella, I think I'm falling in love with you."

The day before, those words would have meant everything to her. But losing the kids had changed her. Being loved by Charlie was still a huge deal, but there were some things she needed to spell out to him.

"I love you, too, Charlie." It was easy to admit, because she'd known for a while now. "But it's complicated. Because of Josh and Kelsey." She stared at his profile, wondering why nothing could be easy for her. Was happily ever after a destination, or just a process?

"The best for me has to be the best for them, as well, Charlie. This running away—well, I feel as if they're running away from me, and not just running toward Gordon. I've been so over-whelmed by everything, I didn't realize how un-safe they must feel." She hadn't recognized it herself until right now. "They don't trust me to manage their lives. Kelsey blames me for driving Gordon away. Josh figures I screwed up, telling Mae and Oscar not to come around unless they could get along. My kids aren't nearly ready to accept you and me as a couple, and I have no idea when they might be. They need time to process everything that's happened to them. Kelsey needs time to figure out that Gordon made a choice that didn't include her. They don't know we're moving in a week, or that Gordon might just turn up like he said. They're going to have to get used to a different house, different school. Different life."

Charlie sounded annoyed. "I wasn't exactly suggesting we drop in to the nearest courthouse and visit the justice of the peace, Bella. Sure, down the line I want something permanent for us. But for right now, can't we go on the way we have been?"

"You mean arguing about everything while we work ourselves to a frazzle doing home improvements on terrible houses?"

He shot her an amused look. "Sounds good to me. As long as there's a bed in the equation."

She reached over and put her hand on his thigh. She looked past him, at the red Pontiac that had pulled even with them. Her mother was waving.

"That's Mae and Oscar. They're exceeding the speed limit in my car. I can't believe it—are they both actually smiling?"

"And waving. Wave, Bella. Before Oscar broadsides us. He's not exactly watching the road."

She waved madly, and another of Mae's favorite sayings popped into her head. She said, "Will wonders never cease?"

Not to be outdone, Charlie said, "Not until hell freezes over."

They smiled at one another.

The highway stretched in front of them, and wonder of wonders, a watery sun was peeking through the gray clouds. It took Bella a few minutes to figure out what the feeling was that welled up inside of her.

"You know what, Charlie? I think I'm happy." For the first time since her birthday, at least, she saw adventure and opportunity ahead instead of disaster. The rest of her life was beckoning. She looked over at the man beside her, his crooked nose, his mouth with that smile.

He would help her find a place to live. He'd help her move. He'd be there for her and for her children, with his battered old pickup truck and his strong arms and his big heart and his good nature.

"Did I ever tell you I play the harmonica?"

"No kidding. What songs?"

"I'm practicing a new one. It's called 'All You Need Is Love.'"

"You'll have to play it for me."

"Every day, Charlie. And every night."

CHAPTER NINETEEN

Two years later

HAPPILY EVER AFTER was one hell of a lot of work, especially when it involved teenagers, Bella thought with a heavy sigh. Her daughter, the drama queen, was at this very moment doing her job, making certain not a single day passed without a major altercation.

"He just doesn't get it, Mom." Kelsey's eyes shot blue fire as her hands went to her hips. "He's *such* a dinosaur, I can't believe you ever married him."

She totally ignored the fact that the dinosaur Bella had married was three feet away, flat on his back under the kitchen sink, and had ears that worked perfectly.

One of the taps was leaking; in the gracious house they'd bought right after they were married, something was always leaking. Lucky for them that Charlie could fix almost anything—except his stepdaughter's attitude.

Bella said, "But he's a dinosaur who cares about you, right, Charlie?"

Grunts of assent came from under the sink. "Could you hand me that small wrench, honey?"

Bella did so while saying to Kelsey, "If Charlie thinks you shouldn't ride on the back of a motorcycle, it means he's protecting you."

Eye rolls. Martyred sighs. "Gabe is a good driver. He's only ever had that one teensy accident, and it wasn't even his fault."

"Two accidents, Kelsey. What about the time he drove through the road barrier and landed in the river?"

"That wasn't his fault. He couldn't see the stupid barrier in the dark, could he?"

"It's not just Charlie who doesn't want you on the back of that machine, Kelsey. Josh agrees with him, and so does Grandpa. Nana, too. *And so do I.* Read my lips. You are not allowed to go anywhere at any time on the back of Gabriel Lalonde's motorcycle."

"How can you all, like, gang up on me this way?" Huge tears rolled down porcelain cheeks.

Bella knew very well what was coming next, and she wasn't disappointed.

"If my father was here, he wouldn't be this mean. He'd let me ride on motorcycles if I wanted."

Bella didn't reply. There were so many responses she could make to that, the most obvious being, *Your father isn't here, he's in Mexico.*

Gordon had been back exactly once, two years before at Christmas, to return the Volvo and sign the divorce papers. He'd promised Kelsey she could come and visit that March, during spring break. Josh had said he didn't want to go, that he and Oscar had a fishing trip planned. Josh was pretty clear about his father by then, whom he referred to as Gordon, and whom he didn't trust.

Josh was right not to trust him. Gordon had called Kelsey as soon as he was back in Melaque to say that it wasn't a good idea for her to come, he didn't have a place big enough. Maybe in the summer?

That was the spring that Bella and Charlie broke through on the financial front, selling all three of the refurbished shotgun houses within two weeks, getting offers from other real-estate firms and several developers for similar work. So, the moment school was out for the summer, Bella offered to pay for Kelsey and Josh to fly to Mexico and stay in an upscale resort, in order to visit Gordon. Josh grumbled, only agreeing to go so he could keep an eye on Kelsey.

They were gone seven days, and when they came home, Josh was furious. "He's living with the woman who works in the store, and he barely had any time at all for us," he told Oscar, who passed along the news to Bella.

Josh wouldn't talk to her about the trip, and

Kelsey just said, tightly, that it had been "like, *so* fantastic."

According to Oscar, Josh was outraged by Gordon's choice of companion. "She's only two years older than I am, Gramps."

Bella noticed that after the trip Kelsey's letters to Gordon, previously a steady stream, had slowed to a trickle.

Still, every time there was a confrontation, Kelsey resurrected the mythical perfect father who never denied her anything. Bella didn't mention to either Kelsey or Josh that under the terms of the divorce, Gordon was supposed to pay support for his children. Of course, not a cent had ever arrived.

Charlie, bless his generous heart, insisted they were better off without Gordon's money. "It would just screw up our income tax," he'd tell Bella. "We can afford to give them everything they need and most of what they want."

Which was true. Who could have guessed that just through word of mouth, Charlie would become known as a trustworthy, totally honest real-estate man, a species rarer than teeth on a hen? By pointing out to potential buyers roofs that leaked and plumbing that was about to blow, he'd made enough money this past year to buy two more shotgun houses, which he and Bella were repairing.

Charlie was saying now, from under the sink,

"Okay, sweetheart, turn the tap on slowly, and tell me whether or not it's still leaking."

Bella leaned over awkwardly, because her belly got in the way these days, even though it was eight more weeks until the baby would arrive. They hadn't planned on it, she and Charlie. She'd been shocked and embarrassed at first. So much for the reliability of condoms. But Charlie had been so ecstatic that Bella couldn't help but get excited.

"We've had so much practice at parenting, this one will be our chance to do everything perfect," he'd told her. The radiant expression on his face would have signaled his delight, even without words. "It's a blessing, sweetheart. It's the best gift you could ever give me. Thank you."

Josh and Kelsey had been united for once in their response to the news. They were both utterly horrified, appalled at this concrete evidence that Bella and Charlie were still, as Kelsey so delicately put it, "doing it."

"Aren't you, like, too *old?*" she had blurted. And then, "What will I tell Melissa and Beverley?"

"That you'll have a new sister or brother." Bella knew her kids would come around the moment the baby arrived. They both doted on Tom and Niki's twins, Robert and Nell. Who wouldn't? They were adorable.

Niki, being Niki, had insisted on breast-feeding them, a monumental commitment that was still going on—in public places—despite the fact the twins were a year and a half, and talking in clear sentences.

Mae, appalled at this lack of restraint, had also been less than enthusiastic when Bella broke her news. "I don't agree with this older-parent business," she'd sniffed. "You'll be my age by the time the child is twenty, Annabella—have you considered that?"

"Well, Mom, you know what you always say—better late than never."

"Well, I certainly never meant it *that* way."

Charlie's daughter, Emma, wasn't overjoyed, either. But with a steady guy and an overloaded schedule at university, she didn't have time to dwell on her father's eccentricities. Bella hoped that someday she and Emma would become friends, but it hadn't happened just yet.

As for Alice, she no longer spoke to Charlie. She'd never forgiven him for breaking the codependent pattern between them. However, she'd learned to drive, had moved to an apartment and become an active member of MADD—Mothers Against Drunk Drivers. According to Emma, she was both independent and proactive. Bella doubted that Alice would be delighted about their great expectations.

So apart from Bella and Charlie, Oscar was the

only one who was thrilled. "I'll have a chance to watch a grandchild grow up, right from the beginning," he enthused. "Although I'll have to fight with your mother over babysitting rights—you know what she's like." He winked at Bella. "Just kidding."

Bella had resigned herself to the fact that her parents would never get along all that well. They didn't quarrel in front of her anymore, and as far as she could tell, they stuck to her rules and didn't run one another down to Josh and Kelsey. But the hard feelings between them were evident at family gatherings, although they took care to limit themselves to glares and scowls and noises in their throats.

"The water's on, and the tap's not leaking one bit," Bella announced.

"Eureka." Charlie scrambled out and got to his feet.

Kelsey gave him a dirty look and flounced out of the room.

"I'm going to take her to get her learner's license this week, and I'll teach her to drive," he said to Bella, wiping his greasy hands on a rag. "And then I'll find her a decent car," he added, wincing as Kelsey's bedroom door slammed with enough force to rock the house. "Josh has the Pontiac, and if she has her own wheels, she won't be as tempted to climb on somebody else's motorcycle. It was partly Josh's idea." Josh and Charlie were as thick as thieves, Mae often said.

To which Bella always responded, what more could a mother ask of a son and a husband?

Charlie always comes through, Bella thought, watching him scrub his hands. She'd thought she loved him, that day in the truck on the way to pick up the kids.

She had loved him. She just didn't fully understand what could happen when someone you loved became your mate, your partner in all things good and bad. In all things wonderful and not so wonderful.

When you finally knew without a shadow of a doubt that no matter how contrary, how stubborn, how opinionated you might act, he would always make you scrambled eggs, fix your taps, cuddle you in bed and applaud your efforts to play "Love Me Tender" on the harmonica at three in the morning.

When that happened, when you really knew the man you loved meant it when he said he'd be around until you died—then that man became your heart.

* * * * *

Welcome to cowboy country...

Turn the page for a sneak preview of
TEXAS BABY
by
Kathleen O'Brien.
An exciting new title from
Harlequin Superromance for everyone
who loves stories about the West.

Harlequin Superromance—
Where life and love weave together in emotional
and unforgettable ways.

CHAPTER ONE

CHASE TRANSFERRED his gaze to the road and iden-
tified a foreign spot on the horizon. A car. Almost
half a mile away, where the straight, tree-lined
drive met the public road. He could tell it was
coming too fast, but judging the speed of a vehicle
moving straight toward you was tricky.

It wasn't until it was about two hundred yards
away that he realized the driver must be drunk…or
crazy. Or both.

The guy was going maybe sixty. On a private
drive, out here in ranch country, where kids or horses
or tractors or stupid chickens might come darting out
any minute, that was criminal. Chase straightened
from his comfortable slouch and waved his hands.

"Slow down, you fool," he called out. He took
the porch steps quickly and began walking fast
down the driveway.

The car veered oddly, from one lane to another,
then up onto the slight rise of the thick green
spring grass. It just barely missed the fence.

"Slow down, damn it!"

He couldn't see the driver, and he didn't recognize this automobile. It was small and old, and couldn't have cost much even when it was new. It was probably white, but now it needed either a wash or a new paint job or both.

"Damn it, what's wrong with you?"

At the last minute, he had to jump away, because the idiot behind the wheel clearly wasn't going to turn to avoid a collision. He couldn't believe it. The car kept coming, finally slowing a little, but it was too late.

Still going about thirty miles an hour, it slammed into the large, white-brick pillar that marked the front boundaries of the house. The pillar wasn't going to give an inch, so the car had to. The front end folded up like a paper fan.

It seemed to take forever for the car to settle, as if the trauma happened in slow motion, reverberating from the front to the back of the car in ripples of destruction. The front windshield suddenly seemed to ice over with lethal bits of glassy frost. Then the side windows exploded.

The front driver's door wrenched open, as if the car wanted to expel its contents. Metal buckled hideously. Small pieces, like hubcaps and mirrors, skipped and ricocheted insanely across the oyster-shell driveway.

Finally, everything was still. Into the silence, a

plume of steam shot up like a geyser, smelling of rust and heat. Its snake-like hiss almost smothered the low, agonized moan of the driver.

Chase's anger had disappeared. He didn't feel anything but a dull sense of disbelief. Things like this didn't happen in real life. Not in his life. Maybe the sun had actually put him to sleep....

But he was already kneeling beside the car. The driver was a woman. The frosty glass-ice of the windshield was dotted with small flecks of blood. She must have hit it with her head, because just below her hairline a red liquid was seeping out. He touched it. He tried to wipe it away before it reached her eyebrow, though, of course that made no sense at all. Her eyes were shut.

Was she conscious? Did he dare move her? Her dress was covered in glass, and the metal of the car was sticking out lethally in all the wrong places.

Then he remembered, with an intense relief, that every good medical man in the county was here, just behind the house, drinking his champagne. He found his phone and paged Trent.

The woman moaned again.

Alive, then. Thank God for that.

He saw Trent coming toward him, starting out at a lope, but quickly switching to a full run.

"Get Dr. Marchant," Chase called. "Don't bother with 911."

Trent didn't take long to assess the situation. A

fraction of a second, and he began pulling out his cell phone and running toward the house.

The yelling seemed to have roused the woman. She opened her eyes. They were blue and clouded with pain and confusion.

"Chase," she said.

His breath stalled. His head pulled back. "What?"

Her only answer was another moan, and he wondered if he had imagined the word. He reached around her and put his arm behind her shoulders. She was tiny. Probably petite by nature, but surely way too thin. He could feel her shoulder blades pushing against her skin, as fragile as the wishbone in a turkey.

She seemed to have passed out, so he put his other arm under her knees and lifted her out. He tried to avoid the jagged metal, but her skirt caught on a piece and the tearing sound seemed to wake her again.

"No," she said. "Please."

"I'm just trying to help," he said. "It's going to be all right."

She seemed profoundly distressed. She wriggled in his arms, and she was so weak, like a broken bird. It made him feel too big and brutish. And intrusive. As if touching her this way, his bare hands against the warm skin behind her knees, were somehow a transgression.

He wished he could be more delicate. But he smelled gasoline, and he knew it wasn't safe to leave her here.

Finally he heard the sound of voices, as guests began to run around the side of the house, alerted by Trent. Dr. Marchant was at the front, racing toward them as if he were forty instead of seventy. Susannah was right behind him, her green dress floating around her trim legs.

"Please," the woman in his arms murmured again. She looked at him, the expression in her blue eyes lost and bewildered. He wondered if she might be on drugs. Hitting her head on the windshield might account for this unfocused, glazed look, but it couldn't explain the crazy driving.

"Please, put me down. Susannah... The wedding..."

Chase's arms tightened instinctively, and he froze in his tracks. She whimpered, and he realized he might be hurting her. "Say that again?"

"The wedding. I have to stop it."

* * * * *

Be sure to look for TEXAS BABY,
available September 11, 2007,
as well as other fantastic Superromance titles
available in September.